English roses were as out of place in the desert as was Cleo,

Prince Sadik decided. In a land of dark-haired beauties, Cleo Wilson shimmered like an oasis—blond to their brunette, blue-eyed to their brown, and, worse, far too curvy for his sensibilities.

Yes, she resembled an oasis—lush, tempting... like a mirage.

Now she had returned to Bahania. Not to him, but for her sister's wedding. Sadik told himself he didn't care.

After all, she had walked away from his bed—which made him question her intelligence. He was Prince Sadik, and she was a mere woman. She should not have been able to leave him. No woman dared to abandon his bed until ordered to do so.

Except for Cleo.

And in the deepest part of him, he burned....

Dear Reader,

June is busting out all over with this month's exciting lineup!

First up is Annette Broadrick's *But Not For Me*. We asked Annette what kinds of stories she loved, and she admitted that a heroine in love with her boss has always been one of her favorites. In this romance, a reserved administrative assistant falls for her sexy boss, but leaves her position when she receives threatening letters. Well, this boss has another way to keep his beautiful assistant by his side—marry her right away!

Royal Protocol by Christine Flynn is the next installment of the CROWN AND GLORY series. Here, a lovely lady-in-waiting teaches an admiral a thing or two about chemistry. Together, they try to rescue royalty, but end up rescuing each other. And you can never get enough of Susan Mallery's DESERT ROGUES series. In *The Prince & the Pregnant Princess*, a headstrong woman finds out she's pregnant with a seductive sheik's child. How long will it take before she succumbs to his charms and his promise of happily ever after?

In *The Last Wilder*, the fiery conclusion of Janis Reams Hudson's WILDERS OF WYATT COUNTY, a willful heroine on a secret quest winds up in a small town and locks horns with the handsome local sheriff. Cheryl St.John's *Nick All Night* tells the story of a down-on-her-luck woman who returns home and gets a second chance at love with her very distracting next-door neighbor. In Elizabeth Harbison's *Drive Me Wild*, a schoolbus-driving mom struggles to make ends meet, but finds happiness with a former flame who just happens to be her employer!

It's time to enjoy those lazy days of summer. So, grab a seat by the pool and don't forget to bring your stack of emotional tales of love, life and family from Silhouette Special Edition!

Sincerely,

Karen Taylor Richman
Senior Editor

Please address questions and book requests to:
Silhouette Reader Service
U.S.: 3010 Walden Ave., P.O. Box 1325, Buffalo, NY 14269
Canadian: P.O. Box 609, Fort Erie, Ont. L2A 5X3

Susan Mallery

THE PRINCE & THE PREGNANT PRINCESS

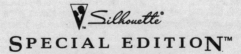

SPECIAL EDITION™

Published by Silhouette Books

America's Publisher of Contemporary Romance

To Liz—you started out as a loyal reader
and became a wonderful friend.

Here's your very own sheik book. With love.

SILHOUETTE BOOKS

ISBN 0-373-24473-8

THE PRINCE & THE PREGNANT PRINCESS

Copyright © 2002 by Susan Macias Redmond

Visit Silhouette at www.eHarlequin.com

Printed in U.S.A.

Chapter One

"His Royal Highness, King Hassan of Bahania, requests the pleasure of your presence at the marriage of his most precious daughter, Princess Zara."

Rather than read any further, Cleo Wilson fingered the thick paper and rubbed the raised lettering of the royal family's crest. How often did a woman like her get an invitation to a royal wedding? Attending would be the social event of a lifetime. She should be wildly excited. Thrilled even. And she would be—just as soon as she stopped having a pressing need to throw up several times a day.

Cleo slumped down in a kitchen chair and thought seriously about banging her head against the table. At least a concussion would be a distraction. Then she reminded herself that she had to stay healthy for the sake of her baby. She rested a hand on her slightly rounded stomach, as if offering comfort and an apology.

"No head banging," she murmured. "I promise to be sensible."

Unfortunately, being sensible meant she had to fly to Bahania for her foster sister's wedding. It meant getting fitted for her maid of honor dress, smiling in such a way that Zara didn't guess there was anything wrong. It also meant keeping her pregnancy from everyone she ran into, most especially the father of her child.

Somehow she didn't think that all the deep breathing in the world was going to help her stress level.

It wasn't supposed to have turned out this way, she reminded herself. At twenty-four she was *supposed* to have her life together. Or at least maintain an illusion of competence and goal setting. She'd even sworn to herself that she wouldn't make the mistake of getting involved with an incredibly inappropriate man ever again. So much for that promise.

Four months ago she'd done the unthinkably stupid. Really. It was so dumb she should win an award. She pictured a nameless master of ceremonies opening a red-lacquered envelope: "The Golden Burro for most inappropriate and really dumb sexual relationship on the planet goes to Cleo Wilson, night manager of a local copy shop who not only slept with a royal prince. She accidentally got pregnant by him."

Two weeks later Cleo flew out of the Spokane airport, en route to Bahania. This trip was very different from the one she'd made nearly six months before with

Zara. Then she and her foster sister had been looking into the unbelievable possibility that Zara might be the illegitimate daughter of King Hassan. While Cleo had been the one encouraging Zara to find out the truth, she'd never thought that her sister might actually be a princess. A relative, yes. Royalty, no.

It had taken a few days in the royal palace, followed by someone actually saying the words *Princess Zara* for Cleo to grasp that the girl she'd once shared a bathroom with was now a member of the Bahanian royal family. While Cleo had been happy for Zara's good fortune, she'd been left feeling as though she was once again on the outside looking in.

They had begun that trip with high hopes, great expectations and cheap, economy-class seats. Now Cleo found herself heading east on a private jet. And not just any private jet. This wasn't some eight-seater, executive-class transportation. Nope, she had an honest-to-goodness Boeing 737 all to herself. Instead of a couple hundred other passengers, there was her, two flight attendants, a pilot, copilot and enough food to feed Rhode Island. She knew because she'd checked out the galley on her exploration of the plane before they'd taken off.

In addition to enough supplies to satisfy all her culinary wants, there were two bedrooms, a living room, a dining room, a workout room, three bathrooms—real bathrooms with showers and space to turn around—along with an office area. Cleo settled in the living room and gazed out the window. Later, when her body clock told her it was her bedtime, she would retire to a real bed and, in theory, arrive in Bahania rested and refreshed.

In reality she would toss and turn all night. The lack of sleep would create charming dark circles under her eyes and the on-going morning sickness would make it impossible to enjoy all the desserts the flight attendants had promised to prepare.

Nearly seventeen hours later, after one quick pit stop for gas, they arrived at the Bahanian International Airport. Cleo collected her overnight case and headed for the ramp. Zara and her fiancé, Rafe, stood waiting at the other end.

Zara threw herself at Cleo and hugged her close. "I've missed you."

"Me, too."

Cleo didn't dare say any more. Unfortunately, her hormones were doing their darnedest to turn her into a babbling, sobbing idiot every time she saw a sappy commercial on television. Who knew what they would do in this circumstance.

Zara hugged her again, then released her and held her at arm's length. "You look great," her sister said.

Cleo laughed. "No. I look like something the cat gacked up. *You* look great."

And of course she did. Zara had been blessed with the finest the gene pool had to offer. As if being tall and model slender wasn't enough, she also had long, dark hair and beautiful brown eyes. Then there was the whole smart-funny-nice thing going on with her. If Cleo didn't adore her sister, she would have backed the car over her years ago.

As they were technically only foster sisters, Cleo

found herself about as far from tall, slender and dark-haired as physically possible. She was short, curvy—okay, plump—with short blond hair that she generally wore sort of spiky. Her lone claim to beauty was her big blue eyes. Zara would say that her big boobs were an asset, too, but Zara would be wrong.

"Hey, little sister," Rafe said, moving in for his greeting.

Rafe Stryker, American hunk, honorary sheik, rich guy and deeply in love with Zara. Cleo sighed. Some girls had all the luck.

She hugged her brother-in-law to be, then fought back hormonal tears.

"Thanks for coming to get me," she said, hating herself for wondering if Sadik had bothered to make the journey to the airport, as well. Not that she had to look around to check. If he'd been there he would have muscled his way to the front and monopolized her attention. He was an arrogant, self-centered, generally annoying guy. So why was she disappointed he hadn't bothered to come say hi?

Zara linked arms with her as they headed out of the royal family's private terminal. Cleo knew that her suitcases would have already been put in the trunk of the waiting limo. If only real life could be this good.

"I'm so glad you're here," Zara said. She motioned for Cleo to slide onto the back seat of the limo first. "The last few months have been hectic. I've been spending time with my father, getting to know him." Zara paused and grinned. "My father. I still can't believe I'm saying that."

"It's pretty great," Cleo said, and meant it. She *was*

happy that Zara had found her father after a lifetime of wondering who he was. If a part of her was envious, she supposed she would learn to live with it. Unfortunately, she happened to know that her father had died before she'd been born. There wasn't going to be the same happy ending in her future.

"Then there is all the wedding stuff." Zara shook her head. "It's been a planning nightmare."

Rafe sat in the seat opposite. "I told her we should elope, but would she listen?"

Zara dismissed him with a wave. "He says that now, but he's pretty excited about the wedding."

Cleo gave her future brother-in-law a doubtful glance. "He doesn't look excited. In fact Rafe looks like he's going to bolt."

"He might want to, but he wouldn't leave me."

Zara's confidence sent a little *ping* of envy bouncing through Cleo's chest. It was intensified when Rafe gave his fiancée a look of such love and devotion that Cleo had to turn away. The moment was too personal and intimate to be shared.

"That's right," he said easily. "Zara's stuck with me for the rest of her life."

That sounded pretty good to Cleo. Oh, not with Rafe. She thought he was nice and all, but he'd never made her heart beat faster. But with someone. All she'd ever wanted was to be the most important person in someone's life. As if that was ever going to happen.

"Tell me about the wedding," Cleo said to change the subject. Her hormones were on overdrive, and she was about three seconds from bursting into tears.

"People are coming from all over the world," Zara

said, shaking her head in bewilderment. "It's crazy, and scary. I like my dress, but the flowers aren't anything I would have picked. Way too big and ornate. But there are certain flowers we have to use and others we can't."

"Tell her about the cake," Rafe said with a wink that promised a fun story.

Zara launched into a convoluted explanation about flavors, colors and size. Cleo tried to pay attention, but part of her had already skipped ahead to arriving at the palace. While she'd been a little disappointed that Sadik hadn't come to the airport, she didn't mind putting off that first meeting. One would think that in the nearly four months they'd been apart she would have been able to recover from a brief two-week affair, but one would be wrong.

She hadn't been able to forget him. Not for a second. So in addition to keeping everyone from finding out she was pregnant, she had to make sure she was cool and indifferent in his presence. She wasn't convinced that was even possible, but she had to try. Not so much for the sake of her pride, but because of the baby.

She didn't know much about Bahanian law, but she suspected everyone would be cranky if they found out she carried Prince Sadik's baby. After all, she was pregnant with a half-royal offspring. Her worst fear was that they would take the child from her.

So she would act completely normal. And in control. With any luck her morning sickness—which did *not* confine itself to morning—would continue to fade. In two short weeks she would be leaving Bahania. She would return home to her regularly scheduled life.

Just her and her baby. No one the wiser. Probably not even her.

The American Federal Reserve chairman had adjusted the Federal Reserve interest rate. Prince Sadik of Bahania had known the adjustment was coming, but that didn't make him like it. The international banking community always became unsettled after such an event.

He tapped a few keys on his computer keyboard, transferring fourteen billion dollars from one account to another, then waited for the confirmation. He would not play in the currency market today. Perhaps not tomorrow either—Sadik only played when he could win.

The confirmation flashed on his screen. He hit the key to send it to the printer, then leaned back in his chair. As much as he hated to admit it, his mind was not on his work. Handling the royal family's private fortune along with consulting with the Bahanian government's finance minister generally kept him well occupied, but not today. Today his mind was on a night of passion that, after four months, should have faded. Unfortunately, it had not.

Even after all this time apart, he could recall every moment he had spent with Cleo.

Sadik rose and crossed to the window overlooking the formal garden that filled the central courtyard of the business wing of the palace. The English roses and hedgerows were as out of place in the desert country as Cleo had been. In a land of dark-haired beauties, Cleo had shimmered like an oasis. Blond to their brunette, fair-skinned to their golden limbs, blue-eyed to their brown. Worse, she was short and far too curvy for his sensibilities. Yes, Cleo was an oasis—lush, tempting and nearly impossible to resist.

Now she had returned. Not to him but for her sister's wedding. He told himself he didn't care, that seeing her again wouldn't bother him. After all, she had walked away from his bed, which made him question her intelligence. He was Prince Sadik of Bahania and she was a mere woman. She should not have been able to leave him. After all no woman dared to abandon his bed until ordered to do so. Except for Cleo.

No matter, he told himself. Her presence in the palace was slightly less than interesting. When she arrived, he would treat her as he would a fly on the wall. As a small annoyance, nothing more. She would be invisible to him. He would not want her. Not ever again.

He returned to his desk and focused his considerable attention on his computer screen. But instead of numbers he saw the body of a woman, and in the deepest part of him he burned.

Cleo walked into the football-field-size foyer of the palace. Everything was as she remembered—huge, luxurious and filled with cats. Parts of the structure dated back nearly a thousand years, and while most of the rooms had been modernized, she still had the sense of stepping into history.

Several of the king's cats stretched out in front of the large window facing the main entrance. Sunlight illuminated the tiled floor.

Zara paused as Cleo looked around. "How does it feel to be back?" she asked her sister.

Cleo studied the floor. It was decorated with a map of the known world...according to fourteenth-century cartographers...detailed in tiny tiles. She rubbed her toe against the boot of Italy.

"There's a dreamlike quality to all this," she admitted. "I can't reconcile standing in a palace in Bahania to my normal life at home."

Zara laughed. "Tell me about it. I have the same feeling, and I've been a permanent resident for nearly four months. Come on. Let's get you settled. I'm in the suite of rooms I was in before. I hope you still want to share space." Zara's expression turned wistful. "I've missed having you around, Cleo."

"I've missed you, too."

Rafe walked into the foyer. He held her two carry-on bags. "I'll have these delivered."

Cleo chuckled. "Rafe, I know they're not heavy. Or is it too demeaning for a powerful sheik to carry luggage?"

"Neither. I'm not allowed near Zara's room."

Zara's good humor returned. She led Cleo toward the main hallway. "The king has been very clear about his desire to keep us separate these last few weeks before we get married. I'm guessing he doesn't want me delivering a baby only seven months after the wedding. Rafe and I managed to sneak away a month ago when we spent that week in London, but since then..." She shrugged. "Let's just say my fiancé is getting the tiniest bit crabby."

Cleo tried to laugh along, but Zara's crack about

getting pregnant had hit a little too close to home. What would her sister say if she knew the truth? What would the king say? She shivered slightly, not wanting to go down that road. It was important that she remember to—

The hairs on the back of her neck stood up. She and Zara were walking down a long corridor that led to the east wing of the palace. Behind them two servants trailed along with Cleo's luggage. Zara continued to talk about the wedding.

Cleo stopped suddenly and turned. A door opened and a man, a tall man, stepped out from behind it. He walked purposefully, as if he knew exactly where he was going. As if he knew she was standing there.

Sadik.

Cleo sucked in a breath. Her heart seemed to flutter in her chest, and adrenaline poured through her. She tried to remain calm—for the baby, if nothing else—but it was impossible. Every nerve in her body went on alert. She couldn't see or hear anyone but him.

An unbearable combination of pleasure and pain filled her. Pleasure at seeing him again and pain for how much she'd missed him in the time they'd been apart.

He approached slowly, steadily, as if she were prey he stalked. The man was impossible, she thought frantically. Impossibly tall, impossibly good-looking, impossibly tempting in bed.

The last time she'd been here, desire had overwhelmed good sense. She had hoped that her months away would have given her a little more backbone. Obviously, she'd hoped in vain. Her first impulse was to throw herself into his arms and beg him to take her right there up against the wall in front of God and everyone. Her second impulse was to run.

Sadik paused in front of her. His perfectly tailored suit probably cost more than she'd made in the past couple of months. She didn't doubt his shoes cost more than her yearly rent. She had nothing in common with this man, and forgetting that would only lead to heartache.

"Cleo," he said. His low, sexy voice made her break out in goose bumps.

"Sadik. Nice to see you." She tried for a casual smile and had a feeling that she fell short. Oh, well.

His dark gaze swept over her, starting at the top of her head where he frowned slightly at her spiky blond hair, past her face to her body where he lingered on her breasts and hips.

She didn't have anyone's ideal of the perfect figure, unless one studied Rubensian paintings, yet Prince Sadik had made it very clear that he found every inch of her desirable. Even now, just looking at her, he spoke his pleasure in her curves and softness. His desire made her melt. She wanted to beg him to pick up where they'd left off. A last flicker of common sense kept her silent.

Aside from the fact that getting involved with him again would be incredibly stupid, one look at her naked body would tell him there had been some pretty significant changes since they'd last done the wild thing.

A muscle twitched in his jaw. It was a small betrayal of his tension, but it gave Cleo courage. At least she wasn't the only one hanging on by a thread.

He nodded at Zara, then turned on his heel and returned the way he had come. Cleo was left with the feeling that he'd wanted to check her out—maybe to see if their passion was alive and well, which it was. She wasn't sure if he'd found that good or bad news.

Chapter Two

"Well?" Zara asked when they resumed their stroll to the guest quarters. "Any sparks left between you two?"

"Not really," Cleo lied. "I mean, dating a prince was interesting the first time around, but it's so not me." She forced herself to smile. "I'm hardly princess material."

"You could be."

"On what planet?"

Zara smiled. "Okay, I get your point. Fitting in here isn't that easy, and believe me, I've been trying for the past four months. I guess the rich and powerful really are different."

Cleo couldn't help laughing. "Zara, you're the college professor in the family and you *just now* figured that out? There's something wrong with you."

Zara grinned. "Hey, I'm a princess. You can't talk to me like that."

"Excuse me, but I'm your sister. I can do whatever I want."

Zara sighed and linked arms with Cleo. "I've missed you so much. It's so great to have you here. I finally feel as if I have someone on my side in this crazy place. It's taken a whole lot longer to adjust than I would have thought."

"Why are you surprised? You went from being a small-town girl to living in a royal palace, halfway around the world. Oh, and you happened to find your long-lost father and fall in love. That's hardly a situation designed to make you feel normal."

"Agreed. While it's nice to finally find roots, I have to admit I spend most of my time with my head spinning."

Cleo didn't doubt it. Just walking the corridors of the royal palace was enough to upset anyone's equilibrium. They moved past bubbling marble fountains and priceless tapestries. There were statues, paintings, open courtyards, alcoves, anterooms and servants. There were also King Hassan's cats who were allowed to go anywhere in the palace by royal order of the king. It was not a world designed to make one feel grounded.

"At first I envied you this," Cleo admitted. "But now I'm not so sure I'd want to be a member of the royal family."

"You'd get used to it."

"Maybe."

Cleo knew that it didn't matter one way or the other. If all went well, she would be out of here in a couple of weeks. As for her own personal fantasy of home, hearth and family…that wasn't going to happen.

She shook off her sad feelings before they could blossom into a full-fledged pity party. No time for that, she reminded herself. This was Zara's special time, and she was determined to do everything she could to make it wonderful.

She glanced at her sister and raised her eyebrows. "Don't forget your promise. I want first chance at all your jewelry castoffs. Anytime you get tired of your diamonds or sapphires, pass them my way."

Zara laughed. "I promise. And if I find an old tiara lying around somewhere, I'll send it over."

Cleo fingered her short, spiky hair. "I'd look good in a tiara. Maybe it would make me look taller." She had a sudden image of herself at her job in Spokane. There she would be, manning the copy machine, dressed in jeans, a sweatshirt and a tiara. It would certainly get the customers talking.

The image was both comical and tragic. Fortunately, they reached their room before hormones could overwhelm her. She might be able to explain her slight weight gain, but sudden bouts of sobbing would definitely get Zara's attention.

Zara opened the door to the suite and stepped inside. Cleo walked into the open space.

"It's just like I remember," she said, taking in the cream-colored walls and the floor-to-ceiling glass windows and doors with a view of the Arabian Sea. The water was as beautiful as she remembered.

"Not bad," she said, glancing at the deep-blue-and-rose tapestries decorating the walls, and the comfortable sofas and chairs that made up a large seating area in the center of the room.

"Everything is as you left it," Zara said, pointing to the right.

Cleo walked toward the room she'd called home for a couple of weeks. This time she was prepared for the luxury of the four-poster bed in the center of the room. She had double French doors that led out onto the balcony that circled the entire palace. An oversize armoire held a television and DVD unit. If she remembered correctly, the bathroom was stocked with enough shampoo, lotions and soaps to fill a boutique.

"Nice work if you can get it," she murmured under her breath.

She recalled the last time she'd been here. Everything had overwhelmed her. Zara had been the prodigal daughter, while she had been out of place. Now she was the not-quite-sister of the bride. Four months ago she'd been on the adventure of a lifetime. Now she was in dangerous territory with a whole lot more to lose.

Zara leaned against the door frame. "You're looking serious. Should I be worried?"

Cleo forced herself to smile. "No. Everything is great. I hope Rafe is prepared to give you surroundings this nice after you're married."

Zara's eyes sparkled with humor. "I've told him that my father has set very high standards. He's going to have to scramble to keep up." Her expression softened. "Cleo, no offense, but you look exhausted. Do you want to crawl into bed and not worry about anything until tomorrow?''

Cleo nodded gratefully. Pregnancy had zapped most of her energy. ''I didn't sleep on the plane last night. Between getting ready to go on vacation and closing up my apartment, I didn't get much rest the night before. So I'm pretty tired. Would you mind if I just hid out until morning?''

''Not at all.'' Zara walked over and hugged her. ''Thanks for coming. I couldn't have gotten through this without you.''

''I wouldn't have missed it for the world.''

Cleo spoke the truth. She knew the danger of returning to Bahania. If anyone found out about her pregnancy, she was in deep trouble. But staying away would have meant disappointing Zara, and Cleo couldn't do that. Not after all they'd been through together.

The downside of taking a nap was being unable to sleep when one wanted to. Cleo turned over in bed and stared at the clock. It was nearly midnight and she felt more restless than tired. Maybe a snack would help. Or even just breathing in the sea-scented air.

After wrapping herself in her robe, she walked barefoot into the living room of the suite she and Zara once again shared. Her sister had arranged for a tray to be delivered around seven that evening. Cleo had taken two bites and had promptly thrown it all up. Now she nibbled cautiously on a sandwich half. It tasted good, and the knot in her stomach seemed to ease.

There wasn't any light showing in Zara's room. Cleo

wondered if her sister had returned from her evening dining with the family or if she was out with Rafe. Maybe the two of them had managed to sneak off together. Cleo sighed. Zara and Rafe looked blissfully happy together. While she was glad her sister had found the man of her dreams, she couldn't help wishing a little of that fairy dust had been sprinkled in her direction. But no. Instead of true love, she'd found a quickie affair with a prince who might still want her but had obviously done just fine without her in the four months she'd been gone. After all, he hadn't tried even once to get in touch with her.

Don't think about that, she told herself. Think about something cheerful, like the fact that her stomach had settled down. She ate the rest of the sandwich half and washed it down with a glass of water. Next she sampled the fruit, which was exotic and delicious.

Feeling almost cheerful, she headed for her bathroom, where she brushed her teeth and tried to figure out if someone could tell she was pregnant just by looking at her face. Fortunately, no one had tattooed a sign to her forehead. She was safe, for the moment.

Cleo returned to her bedroom but still didn't feel sleepy, so she headed out onto the balcony. The French doors opened easily. As she stepped into the coolness of the autumn evening, she inhaled the sweet scents of the flowers in the garden, along with the salty smell of the ocean. Back home the leaves were turning as winter beckoned, but here the days were balmy and beautiful.

She could hear the chirps and clicks of night creatures, along with the faint sounds from the waves. Just like a dream, she thought with a lazy smile. Only, this time she knew that dreams could occasionally have unhappy endings. The last time she'd stood on this balcony alone in the night, she'd wished for a handsome prince with whom to share the moment. Now she knew better. Handsome princes were great guys...from a safe distance.

An out-of-place sound caught her attention. She turned and saw someone moving in the shadows. Her heart jumped. Not out of fear but out of recognition. She didn't have to see his face to recognize the man. Speak of the devil.

Sadik walked toward her, moving into the light of the small lamp just to the left of her bedroom door. He didn't say anything as he approached, which was just as well, for her throat had gone dry at the sight of him.

He wore jeans and a polo shirt—casual dress. There was nothing unusual about that, except Sadik was a prince and she'd never seen him in anything but a business suit or a tuxedo. Or in nothing at all.

Don't go there, she told herself. Thinking about Sadik being naked was incredibly dangerous...especially given her current circumstances.

He stopped less than two feet from her. His expression didn't give anything away, but she had the distinct impression he wasn't happy to see her. He stood at least six feet tall, which meant it was too darned easy for him to tower over her.

A trickle of apprehension made her want to step back. Rather than give in, she did what she always did best. Think with her mouth.

"I have to say, you loom better than anyone I know," Cleo said, leaning against the railing and striving for casual. "Is it something tall men do instinctively or is it more of a princely art?"

His gaze narrowed. "You still have not learned to curb your tongue. As a woman, you should know better."

She rolled her eyes. "You left out the word *mere,* and that's what really gives the sentence its spice. As a *mere* woman, I should know better."

"Exactly."

His agreement didn't make her feel very charitable or friendly. "Sadik, you've got to get some different material. It's the new millennium. Women now have brains and we use them. Or didn't you get the memo?"

He seemed to loom a little more aggressively. "I am Prince Sadik of Bahania. You will not speak to me this way. You must learn your place."

"Last time I checked, my place was about ten feet away." She nodded toward her room. "So I do know it, and I have to say, it's lovely."

He took a half step closer, which made him way too close. Then he glared at her and growled. Cleo couldn't believe it. There was an honest-to-goodness growling noise in his throat.

A shiver tripped up her spine and made her shiver. On the one hand she was pleased to know that she could still bug him. On the other hand, being this close to him made it hard to think and to breathe. Not a good combination.

He glared at her, and she glared right back. No way was she going to let him know how much he'd hurt her. There had been at least 120 nights since she'd last seen him, and she would bet she'd cried herself to sleep at least seventy of them. Which made her mad at both him and herself.

The trick was to make sure he never found out that he had ever mattered. Oh, and not to let him know she was pregnant.

"When do you plan to apologize for leaving my bed?" he asked.

The question stunned her. She stared at him for several seconds as the words chased themselves around in her head. Was he crazy? It was a horrible time to suddenly remember she wore panties, a nightgown and a robe. Little protection against Sadik's masculine charms.

"I have nothing to apologize for. I was ready to end things, so I left."

The muscle in his jaw tightened. "No woman leaves my bed without being asked."

His arrogance really got on her nerves. "Apparently that's not completely true, as I left before you asked. And while we're on the subject of apologies, where's mine?"

The tight jaw muscles twitched. "For what?"

He spoke through clenched teeth. It was a neat trick, she thought.

"Why am I not surprised that you don't get it," she said more to herself than to him. "It's so typically male." She folded her arms over her chest and glared at him. "You gave me jewelry, Sadik. After we made love, you offered me expensive gifts. It's not like we had an actual relationship and cared about each other." Okay, she'd cared about him, but he didn't have to know that. "It was a little too much like leaving money on the nightstand. I may not be a royal princess, but that's no excuse to offer payment for services.''

She had the pleasure of seeing Sadik look completely stunned. His jaw unclenched, and for a second she thought his mouth might drop open.

''Those gifts were not a payment,'' he said, obviously seething with barely controlled rage. ''They were an expression of my honor at the treasure being offered.''

Cleo had to turn that sentence over a couple of times before it made anything close to sense. By treasure did he actually mean sex? ''In case you hadn't noticed, I wasn't a virgin. There wasn't any treasure involved. Which you knew, by the way, because we talked about it before we—''

He kissed her. Cleo was unprepared, and Sadik moved so quickly she didn't have any warning. One second she'd been talking and the next, he took her in his arms and drew her close.

The feel of his strong body against her own caused all the air to rush from her lungs. She gasped to catch her breath, which left her vulnerable. At least, that's what she told herself when she decided not to put up a struggle as his mouth settled on hers.

It had been too long, she thought hazily, caught in the grip of instant and mind-numbing passion. Every nerve in her body caught fire as sensual heat rushed through her, making her want to tear off her clothes and have him touch her everywhere.

He settled his mouth more firmly on hers, then ran his tongue across her lower lip. Shivers raced up and down her arms. Her extrasensitive breasts swelled uncomfortably. All this and he hadn't even put his tongue in her mouth. She didn't think she would be able to stand that.

He read her mind, she thought, both aroused and distressed as he swept into her mouth. At the first touch she knew she was lost. The familiar pattern of their intimate dance came back to her in a heartbeat. Remembered passion joined present passion, combining, growing, making her strain toward him.

She clung to his broad shoulders, then, unable to help herself, ran her fingers through his thick, dark hair. She could inhale the scent of his body, feel his heat, his arousal. The thought of him being inside of her nearly made her weep with desire.

When he put his hands on her hips, she felt herself drifting away. In a matter of seconds she would be lost. He deepened his kiss as he drew his hands higher, to her waist and up to her rib cage.

Several thoughts flashed through Cleo's mind at once. That she couldn't emotionally risk giving herself to him again. That if he touched her too much, he might figure out the differences in her body. After all, he'd spent hours learning every inch of her to a level of detail that had left her weak and breathless. That her hormones were doing their thing and she was about forty-five seconds away from a sobbing meltdown.

None of the possibilities made her feel safe, so she forced herself to pull away.

Sadik's breathing was as rapid as her own. She was gratified to see the fire of need burning in his dark eyes. At least the wanting hadn't been all one-sided. Neither of them said anything. She suspected they were both waiting for the other person to speak first. She knew he was strong enough to outwait her, although she gave the staring contest a try.

"I'm not doing this," she said at last when it became apparent they could be at it all night. "The only reason I'm here is that my sister is getting married. If you have an itch, I suggest you could find someone else who's actually interested to scratch it for you."

The implication that she wasn't interested was an outright lie, but tough times called for tough measures.

Passion faded from his eyes as anger took its place. He didn't say a word, instead he turned on his heel and stalked away. Cleo slumped against the railing and tried to calm her heart rate. She would say that round had been a draw, which was unfortunate. She really needed a win. She also needed to stay out of trouble.

Instinctively she placed a hand on her stomach. It wasn't Sadik's fault that she was still crazy about him. But regardless of her feelings, she didn't dare give in. The last thing in the world she wanted was for him to find out the truth.

Cleo didn't fall asleep before dawn, so it was nearly ten when she finally stumbled out of bed and into her shower. An hour later she was "taking breakfast" on the balcony outside of her room.

Everyone should start their day this way, she thought happily. Sunlight burned away the shadows from last night. She felt confident there wouldn't be any interruptions from a certain handsome prince because he would have long since started his day, leaving her free to admire the view and enjoy her breakfast.

As she'd already thrown up twice, she was ravenous. Warm scones, fruit and herbal tea tempted her appetite. She leaned back in her chair and sighed with contentment. There were moments when it was good to be a guest of the royal family. The food was delicious, the view incredible and for once her morning sickness hadn't left her feeling too shaky. Actually the morning episodes were the easiest. The ones that struck later in the day left her feeling as if she'd just gone five rounds with a stubborn strain of the flu.

A small price to pay, she thought as she picked up a strawberry and took a bite. At least it was getting better. In the beginning she'd tossed her cookies nearly—

"Good morning."

Cleo glanced up, then quickly sprang to her feet. She swallowed a sudden case of nerves and tried to smile. "Good morning, Your Highness," she said to the king of Bahania.

King Hassan smiled and motioned to the small table the servants had set up for her. "Are you enjoying your breakfast?"

"Yes. Very much. I overslept. Jet lag, I guess."

Hassan nodded. When he didn't keep on walking, Cleo figured this wasn't a morning constitutional. He must have a purpose. She cleared her throat. "Ah, Zara is getting a final fitting on her gown. She should be back in an hour or so."

Hassan motioned to one of the chairs, as if asking permission to join her. Cleo nodded vigorously, feeling like one of those little dogs people put in the back of their cars.

"Please," she said, then fumbling when he paused, as if waiting for her to sit first.

Was she allowed to be seated when he was standing? she wondered. Life was difficult when all her royal training came from umpteen viewings of the movie *The King and I.* It's not as if members of the royal family frequently crowded into her small apartment kitchen.

She finally plunked herself down on her chair and passed a plate of scones. The king took a seat, but declined the scones.

"Please continue with your breakfast," Hassan said as he reached for her pot of tea and poured himself a cup. "How was your trip to Bahania?"

"Long, but otherwise pretty fabulous." She spread jam on her scone. "I really appreciate the use of the family jet. It was a whole lot nicer than my first trip here."

"Not so many people?"

"Exactly."

"I am glad the jet could be of use to you." He smiled kindly.

Cleo ignored a twinge of envy. This man was Zara's father. Cleo was less impressed by the fact that he was a king than that he cared about finding his daughter after not knowing about her for twenty-eight years. Not many men would have been so open and excited at the prospect of a new family member. Still, if good fortune was going to happen to someone, she was glad it was Zara.

"We are happy you have come for the wedding," the king said.

"I wanted to be here." It was only half a lie, Cleo thought.

Hassan smiled. "Zara's happiness would not be complete without the presence of her beloved sister."

Hassan was just a tad under six feet, with graying hair and strong, handsome features. Cleo could see the family resemblance in his sons and daughters. They were all tall, dark and very good-looking. She, on the other hand, was a short, round, baby-chick blonde with blue eyes and a slight inclination to chubby thighs.

"Your Highness, Zara means the world to me, but you must know we're not actually sisters."

The king patted her hand. "You are sisters of the heart. Zara has told me much of your years together. A relationship born of such times runs deep. You honor each other, and as Zara's father, I honor the bond you share. You have come to be with Zara now, because your presence makes her happy. Therefore you make me happy, as well. You are part of our family, Cleo. You will always be welcome here."

Cleo felt as if he'd stabbed her. His complete acceptance made her feel like slime. Not only was she carrying his unborn grandchild, she had planned to duck out of the country without anyone knowing the truth.

Her conscience wrestled with reality. If the king knew about the baby, he would want to keep it in Bahania. Cleo knew she didn't belong here, which meant she might lose her child. Zara had the genes to be a member of the royal family, but Cleo wasn't so lucky.

"You must tour the garden," the king said, as if he wasn't aware of the battle raging inside of her. "When you were last here, the fierce summer daunted many of our most beautiful plants. However, in the fall, they come out and show off their glory.''

She was grateful for the change in subject. ''I'll make it a point to go look at them,'' she said. ''I enjoyed the gardens before.''

''They're even more beautiful now. Many things bloom here in Bahania.''

She glanced at him, but despite his cryptic words, he seemed to speak only of the wildlife. There was no way he could have guessed, she told herself as a shiver of unease rippled through her. She was overreacting.

Hassan spoke of his precious cats for a few minutes, then rose to his feet. ''Unfortunately, duty calls,'' he said. ''Otherwise I would like to spend more time with you.'' He touched her shoulder. ''Welcome, Cleo. We are all happy to have you with us. Stay as long as you would like. I know that you have a life back in America, but should you wish to make your home here in Bahania, we would be most honored.''

He nodded slightly, then left.

Cleo stared after him. It was only when she sniffed that she realized tears rolled down her face. She wiped her cheeks with her napkin. There was no point in blaming this outburst on her hormones. Hassan's acceptance had opened an old wound—that of wanting to belong to a person, a family, even a place.

Despite his kindness, it wasn't going to happen here, she reminded herself. That particular fantasy was going to have to be fulfilled somewhere else.

Maybe it was time to make a change in her life, she

thought as she headed back to her room. When she went home after Zara's wedding, she would evaluate her situation and find a way to feel, if not happiness, then at least contentment.

Chapter Three

Sadik listened as the financial minister from El Bahar outlined the financing proposal for the proposed air force the two countries were developing. The representative from the City of Thieves was also in attendance. The two countries, along with the City of Thieves, worked together to protect the oil fields deep in the desert. The air force was a large part of their plans to modernize security arrangements.

Each reconnaissance plane cost many millions of dollars, while the fighters' price tag could top a hundred million dollars. Under normal circumstances, Sadik would be crunching the numbers in his head faster than any calculator and asking dozens of questions.

These were not normal circumstances.

He couldn't stop thinking about Cleo. She haunted

his mind like a ghost haunting a castle. Ever moving, never appearing in the same place twice, disappearing for a time, then reappearing when he least expected to see her.

He ached for her. Their time apart had not seemed to dull his passion, nor had it allowed him to forget her. She was more beautiful than he remembered…and more tempting. Her lush body, her blond hair and blue eyes—there wasn't a part of her he didn't want. Kissing her had been a mistake. It had given him a taste of the paradise he'd had before, and he desperately wanted to go there again.

He wanted to make love with her. He wanted to explore every curve, every hollow. He wanted to taste her and touch her, drive her mad, force her to surrender so that he could take her again and again.

"Your Highness, do you agree?"

Sadik stared at the minister sitting across from him. He had no idea what they were discussing. Anger surged. How dare Cleo invade his mind and keep him from his duties? He loved his work with a passion he had never felt for a mere woman. There was no reason for him to be so distracted. In time he would have Cleo again. Until then he would forget about her.

But the simple words did nothing to ease the pounding need inside of him, nor did they improve his memory or his attention span.

"I apologize, Minister," he said curtly. "Would you repeat the question?"

"We were discussing the options for providing training. There are several companies making bids. In addition both the British and the Americans have offered to send pilots to train our troops.''

''First we must agree on the aircraft,'' Sadik said. He allowed himself one last image of Cleo, then pushed her from his mind. Now was the time to work.

''I'm glad this isn't going to be a formal dinner,'' Zara said, flopping down on the sofa and sighing. ''I hate those state functions that go on for hours. They can be incredibly boring.''

''How many people will be attending tonight?'' Cleo asked. The more the merrier, she thought glumly. Each person in the room was a potential buffer between her and Sadik. As much as she tried to forget it, his kiss from the previous night still haunted her. She found herself alternating between the need to run for cover and the desire to seek him out and finish what they'd started.

''I'm not sure. A couple hundred.'' Zara shrugged. ''As far as the inner circle of the royal family, it will be us, of course, and the king. Sadik is the only prince in the palace right now. Prince Reyhan is off at an oil conference somewhere. The crown prince is doing crown princely duties in central Africa. Don't ask me what. And Prince Jefri is in El Bahar talking with the king there about the joint air force.''

Cleo stared at her sister in amazement. ''Listen to yourself,'' she said.

''What?''

Cleo reached to her right and pulled loose a small pillow. She threw it at Zara. ''You're casually discussing the whereabouts of several members of the royal family. Doesn't that strike you as the least bit odd? You're a member of a ruling family. You're an honest-to-goodness princess, Zara. How can you be so calm about this?''

Zara angled toward her. She wore a stylish short-sleeved dress that screamed designer. A large diamond glittered on her left hand. Her always beautiful hair was sleek and shiny—the result of expensive hair treatments and an even more expensive stylist on call.

''I'm not calm,'' Zara admitted, her large eyes dark and troubled. ''I feel weird about it all the time. But if I gave in to those feelings, I'm afraid I would end up curled up in a closet, rocking and making weird noises.''

Cleo laughed. ''Not an attractive visual.''

''Exactly.'' Zara fingered her gold hoop earrings. ''I didn't set out to be a princess. I just wanted to find my father. He happens to be the king of Bahania. Just between the two of us, I wish he'd been a normal guy, but he's not. I'm here, so you have to be here, too.''

''The difference is, I get to run away when all this becomes too much.''

''I envy you that,'' Zara said.

''No, you don't. You want to be with Rafe.''

Her sister's expression changed to complete happiness. ''You're right. I'll put up with anything, even being a princess, just to be near him.''

''I envy you that,'' Cleo said easily, knowing Zara would understand.

''You'll find someone,'' her sister told her.

Cleo wasn't so sure.

''If it wasn't for Rafe, I'd miss my old life a lot

more," Zara said after a couple of minutes of silence. "I still miss teaching at the university. Plus my friends. No one but you is coming to the wedding. I wanted to offer to pay for the plane tickets, but I knew people would take that wrong." She stretched her hand across the back of the sofa and touched Cleo's shoulder. "Thank you for coming."

"I wouldn't have missed it for anything," Cleo told her truthfully.

Zara cleared her throat. "You know, there are a lot of opportunities in the city. The economy here is expanding and there's always plenty of work."

Cleo knew exactly where she was going. "Thanks for the suggestion, but I don't think I'd fit in. I don't exactly look like a local, plus, who's going to hire the almost relative of the royal family?" She forced herself to laugh. "We'll just have to do e-mail a lot."

"I guess." Zara's answering smile faded. "Cleo, why did you run off so suddenly before? You still had a few days of vacation left, but you headed for home without warning."

"I'm sorry about that. I just—" How to balance the truth with the need to keep her secret. "It was a lot of things. I could see that you needed time to bond with your new family. I wasn't a part of that. Not only was I afraid of getting in the way, I didn't exactly fit in."

"You could never be in the way. I love you and I like having you around. I think the king has a soft spot for you, too."

"He's been very kind," Cleo admitted, suddenly fighting tears. Pregnancy was the pits, she thought as she sniffed. "But I do have my own life back in Spokane."

"Was Sadik part of your decision to leave?"

Cleo swallowed. "He was a lot of fun, but our relationship wasn't anything important." All lies, she thought, feeling guilty. Or maybe only half lies. She suspected their relationship hadn't meant anything to Sadik. "We had a fling, and then it ended. It happens all the time, although probably more with him than with me."

"He's very good-looking."

"I actually figured that out on my own. But come on. Me and a prince?" Cleo forced out a laugh. "Can you see *that* ever happening?"

Her heart hurt so much it was difficult to breathe. She desperately wanted Zara to protest, to say that of course everything would work out with Sadik, but that wasn't going to happen. Zara didn't have enough information to figure out what Cleo needed to hear, and even if she did, she wouldn't lie.

Zara laughed, too. "I guess you're right. He's pretty arrogant."

"I'm beginning to think that all princes are arrogant. It must be part of the training."

Zara fingered her skirt. "Do you mind very much about Rafe? I mean that I'm marrying him?"

"No." At least in this, Cleo could tell the truth. "You two are so in love. That makes me happy. You deserve someone wonderful in your life. I'm sorry we're going to be living so far apart, but we can make that work. We'll still be emotionally close, and you can tell me all about life with a sheik."

Zara grinned. "I never thought I would be marrying a sheik. In his heart Rafe will always be American, which helps. He loves the desert, and the City of Thieves is amazing. He's taken me there a couple of times. There's so much history. I can't wait to start exploring and studying."

"That will keep you busy. Then you start having babies. You're going to have a good life."

"I hope so," Zara admitted.

Cleo continued to smile, even though the tears threatened again. It's not that she didn't want Zara to be happy, but was it so wrong to want the same for herself?

She reminded herself that the best way to get through all this was to act normal and leave as quickly as possible after the wedding. Like the next day. The sooner she was back in the States, the safer she would feel.

Her stomach lurched slightly. Cleo gritted her teeth. Please, God, let her not throw up at that night's dinner. Formal event or not, tossing her cookies would give everyone something to talk about and that's exactly what she didn't need.

Cleo stood at the entrance of the reception room. Her stomach was surprisingly calm, considering how nervous she felt. Nearly two hundred people were sipping cocktails and chatting with each other. The combined value of the clothing and jewelry was probably enough to match the gross national product of a small country. Cleo glanced down at her new finery, compliments of Zara, who had invited a couple of boutique owners to bring in their wares and then told Cleo to choose a new wardrobe.

The designer dress she wore wasn't anyone's idea of a castoff, yet Cleo couldn't escape the sensation of once again being a charity case. Funny how she thought she'd left that behind her years ago. Since she'd moved out at eighteen, she'd been making her own way and paying her bills on time. She even had a nest egg, although by royal family standards, it was amazingly pitiful. But it was enough for her. The problem was, she couldn't afford to keep up with the elite social circles in Bahania, and Zara knew it.

Four months ago Zara had been the one feeling weird about accepting gifts of clothing from her newly found father. Cleo had seen their time here as an adventure. Now she shared Zara's reluctance. Did carrying Sadik's baby make all that much difference?

Dumb question, she told herself as she headed for the bar. Her midnight-blue beaded dress swished as she walked. High-heeled gold pumps gave her a couple of inches of height, but what she liked best about her outfit was the loose style. It hinted at curves without actually hugging them. So far no one had noticed her bulging belly and she planned to keep it that way.

"Club soda," she said when the bartender looked up.

She took the glass he offered and turned to survey the room. So these were the beautiful people, she thought as she sipped on her drink. They were certainly out of her league. If she had to make idle chitchat she would—

"I fear you grow more beautiful each time I see you."

The wrapped-in-velvet voice made her tremble. She didn't have to turn around to know who stood there.

"I didn't think royal princes feared anything." She glanced to her left and saw that Sadik had joined her. He looked fabulous in a tailored black tuxedo. It reminded her of the first time they'd met—when she'd taken one look at him and lost most of her common sense, not to mention a good part of her heart.

He took her free hand in his, brought it to his mouth and kissed her knuckles. It was a courtly gesture that belonged to another time and place. Darn the man—it worked, anyway. She felt herself melting.

"So what's new, Sadik?" she asked, determined to act completely normal. "How's the stock market?"

"We do well."

She didn't bother asking how many billions he'd made that day. Sadik had a relationship with numbers that was completely foreign to her. She knew he had tripled the personal fortune of the family in fewer than six years. Given the uncertain world-economic situation, that bordered on a miracle.

"Are you excited about the wedding?" she asked, mostly because she couldn't think of anything brilliant to say.

"My new sister seems happy with her choice in groom. Rafe is a good man. They are well matched."

"She must be relieved to know she has your blessing. I know the uncertainty of getting it was keeping her up nights."

His gaze narrowed. "Even now you defy me. Why do you play a game you can't win?"

"I'm not interested enough to play with you anymore. As for winning—it wasn't very interesting when I won last time."

He sucked in a breath. "I was the victor."

He had been, too. He'd seduced her in a heartbeat and had left her begging for more. Not that she was going to admit that to him. "Whatever. I really don't remember."

He put his hand on her shoulder and stroked the side of her neck. Had she been one of the king's pet cats, she would have purred.

"Your mouth tells lies, but I see the truth in your eyes. The passion is as it always was between us. Your attempts to resist me will only make us both more hungry."

"You managed to forget about me for the four months I was gone, Sadik. The fact that you're paying attention to me now simply means that I've turned up on your radar. It's a knee-jerk reaction that isn't the least bit flattering—nor am I interested."

She had more to say, but at that moment she was saved by the bell…literally. The head butler rang a gong that announced it was time for dinner. Cleo took the opportunity to duck away from Sadik before he could trap her with him.

How could she have blurted that out to him? If he had a single, functioning brain cell—and she happened to know he had more than the average working guy—he would figure out that her feelings were hurt by the fact that he'd let her go and hadn't once bothered to get in touch with her. She didn't want him thinking that he mattered. She didn't want him thinking about her at all. He already had too much power over her sexually. The last thing she needed was him using her fragile emotions against her, too.

She walked into the main dining room and had a moment of panic at the thought that they might be seated next to each other. Several long tables filled the smaller of the formal dining rooms in the palace. Cleo found her name on the seating chart, then drew in a relieved breath when she saw the seats next to her were already taken. Rafe sat on her right, which meant Zara was next to him. A least she would be close to a semi-family member. On her left was a man she didn't know, but he seemed friendly enough when he greeted her and held out her chair.

"Jonathan Grant," he said easily, holding out his hand.

"Cleo Wilson," she said, and settled in her chair. Rafe turned and gave her a wink before returning his attention to Zara.

Cleo took a moment to glance around the room. During her first stay in the palace, she'd explored several of the public rooms. She'd even almost begun to understand the floor plan. This particular dining room was used for smaller formal events. The wall tapestries dated back to the fifteenth century and showed the various explorers who had made their way to Bahania. Four marble statues stood in the corners. At the far end of the room was a raised dais for a small orchestra. Several crystal chandeliers provided light.

Everything glittered, especially the well-dressed people. How happy they must be that the king agreed to keep his cats out of the room on evenings such as these.

"What's so funny?" Jonathan asked.

He was an attractive man in his late forties. Cleo picked up her water glass. "I was thinking that a couple of loose cats could do a lot of damage with their shedding in this group."

Jonathan grinned. "I'm still picking off hairs from my last visit here. Black suit, white cat. I swear I heard her laughing as she rubbed against me."

Cleo chuckled at the image. As she did so, she felt something intense, as if...

She raised her head. Sadik might not be next to her, but he was across from her. The table was wide enough to keep them from talking easily, but that didn't matter. It was enough to know he was *there*. There and watching her. She deliberately turned back to her seatmate.

"What business brings you to Bahania?" she asked.

Jonathan looked faintly surprised at the question. "I'm the American ambassador."

Heat instantly flared on her cheeks. She wanted to crawl under the table. "Sorry, I didn't know. I don't actually live in Bahania and, well..." Her voice trailed off. Did it matter that she didn't live here? Her circle of friends had never included an ambassador.

"I should have done a better job of introducing myself," he said easily. "As your sister is Princess Zara, I assumed you would have been told about me."

So he knew who she was. Figures. Life could be annoyingly unfair. "So far Zara and I have pretty much talked about the wedding. You know—girl stuff."

"I have three daughters so I know exactly what you're talking about."

The fact that he had children made her able to put aside her faux pas. As dinner was served, she found herself chatting easily with Jonathan. He explained that his wife had returned home to the States to get their oldest settled at college and visit family.

All through the various courses Cleo did her best to ignore Sadik's watchful gaze. He was polite enough to converse with the women on either side of him, but she would have bet he barely heard what they were saying. He was too busy glaring at her.

When the dessert plates had been cleared away, the waiters brought out trays of open champagne bottles. The bubbly liquid was served, and King Hassan rose to toast his daughter.

Cleo joined in the applause and, at the appropriate time, raised her glass to her lips but was careful not to swallow. Conflicting emotions swelled up inside of her. She was deeply happy for her sister. Zara deserved all her joy. But the knowledge that things would never be the same between them made Cleo feel hollow inside.

The king ended the meal by inviting everyone to dance in the main ballroom. As Cleo pushed back her seat, she could already hear the strains of music. But with her heavy heart and suddenly unsettled stomach, what she wanted more than anything was to hurry back to her room for a quiet pity party and a good movie. She nearly made it to the far door before she was caught.

"The American ambassador is happily married."

Cleo spun toward Sadik. "Number one, stop sneaking up on me. It's annoying. Number two, I know all about Jonathan's wife and his daughters. We had a lovely time chatting together and don't you dare turn it into something sleazy.''

His dark eyes were unreadable. A muscle twitched in his jaw. She half expected him to throw her over his shoulder and spirit her away. A part of her would have welcomed being in his bed, regardless of the price. Fortunately, all he did was lead her toward the ballroom, then pull her into his arms for a dance.

They moved without speaking. Cleo let herself relax to the rhythm of the music. Maybe it was madness, but being with Sadik felt like coming home.

Despite the height difference, they danced well together. She easily anticipated his moves. The heat from his body made her feel safe.

Safe, she thought sadly. There was a unique concept. She might be many things with the prince, but the least of them was safe.

''You should go bother a skinny, tall brunette and leave me alone,'' she grumbled.

''You should stop talking. You're spoiling our moment together.''

''Is that what we're having?''

''Yes. And you're enjoying it. Besides, I want no other woman but you.''

His words sank down to her heart, ripping away protective layers of common sense. She knew he was only talking about sex, but she couldn't help wishing…wanting…something more. Sadik held her close enough that she could feel the call of his body. She took the half step closer, nestling herself against him. His only response was to sigh softly.

For a time, with her pregnancy, her breasts had been extremely tender. That symptom had faded so she could now enjoy the sensation of pressing close to his hard chest. Against her will, memories flooded her as she remembered what it had been like to be with him. She recalled the way he'd touched her everywhere. Slowly, almost worshiping her body. He'd made her feel physically perfect.

Cleo closed her eyes in an attempt to ignore the past and the pain it brought. If it was only sex, she could find the will to resist. But she and Sadik had shared so much more. When they had satiated themselves after an hour or two, they had talked. First of inconsequential matters, but eventually they had shared the details of their past. She'd heard about the lonely child growing up in a world of wealth and privilege, ignored by his parents and raised by a nanny, then a tutor. She'd glossed over the first ten years of her life but had told him about going to live with Zara and her mother.

She had allowed herself to believe that she'd gotten past the arrogant shell to the actual man beneath. She'd told herself that she mattered to him. She'd been wrong on both counts.

"Come to me tonight," he breathed in her ear. "We can rediscover paradise together."

Cleo was so tempted she nearly fainted. Knowing that he wanted her made her long to give in. Apparently being around Sadik still made her forget all that was important. She took a half second to try to convince herself that it was okay to be weak and spineless, then she remembered what was at stake.

She did her best to look bored as she raised her gaze to his. "I'm seriously flattered, but I'd rather not. You're a great guy, Sadik, really. But the thing is, I've met someone else. We hooked up shortly after I returned to Spokane."

Sadik raised dark eyebrows. "You have another man in your life? What is his name?"

Her mind went completely blank. Ah…a name. Any name. "Rick. He's in plumbing." Internally she winced. "He's fabulous. We met and it was love at first sight. Really. Right there in front of my kitchen sink." She widened her eyes, hoping for a look of sincerity.

Sadik did not look convinced. "Your sister hasn't mentioned this Rick person."

"I didn't say anything to her. Zara is so caught up in the wedding and everything. I didn't want to distract her." Cleo swallowed. She'd never been a very good liar. Maybe she should have practiced more.

"So it's serious with you and this Rick?"

"Uh-huh. We're practically engaged."

Sadik threw back his head and began to laugh. Cleo wanted to stomp her foot…preferably grinding her heel into his instep.

"I don't see what's so funny," she hissed. "You wanted me. The possibility exists that one other man on the planet might feel the same way."

He stopped laughing and pulled her hard against him. "I do not doubt your charms, Cleo, merely your story. While you are desirable and could have many suitors, you could not be with another man after being with me.''

He spoke with a confidence that made her want to box his ears.

''You make me crazy,'' she told him as she pulled free of his embrace. ''You also have a very high opinion of yourself. Frankly this conversation bores me.''

At least they were on the edge of the dance floor, she thought gratefully as she stalked away. Sadik didn't follow her, but then he hardly had to worry about where she was going to go. The single choice was back to her room. For the forty-seventh time that day, tears filled her eyes. As if throwing up wasn't enough, she'd turned into a faucet. Nothing about this situation was fair.

What made it worse was Sadik had been correct. There was no way she could be with another man after being with him. Somehow she'd bonded herself with him until no other man could possibly matter.

But he only cared about her attentions as some sort of game. He wanted her in his bed, yet not in his life. Cleo hated that. She also didn't want to explore what she wanted, because she had a bad felling that the truth would terrify her. Wishing for the moon was a steep, slick road to heartache. The problem was, she could already feel herself starting to slip.

Chapter Four

Cleo eyed the long tables laden with wrapped presents. Each gift looked beautiful enough to be in a display window, and accompanying each was a letter, a blank form and pages of documentation.

"I'm going to bet there's not a blender in the bunch," she murmured.

Zara carried the first package over to the only empty table. Several chairs had been pulled up around it, along with a stack of file folders.

"If you think this is bad, you should go check out the other gift room. It has the official gifts offered by various governments and heads of state. I'm not even allowed to open those. Apparently, there's an entire protocol staff to see to them. However, after a series of lectures, they finally trusted me to open and log in the private gifts.'' She smiled at Cleo. ''Still want to help?''

''Sure. But first I want to know the difference between 'official' and 'private' gifts.''

Zara handed her the blank form. ''You need to be filling this out while I open. When you get bored, we'll trade. As to the difference, I'm not sure. It's how they're sent or something. I'm just hoping no one gives us a pair of elephants.''

Cleo started to laugh. ''You're not talking about matching statuary, are you?''

''Nope. The king keeps swearing it's a time-honored gift to a marrying couple. Something about fertility or long life, or maybe both. I could handle a small dog or a bird, but I don't want to be responsible for any elephants.''

Cleo reached for the paperwork. ''This one is from a former U.S. president.'' She started writing on the form, filling in the spaces for who the gift was from and the date opened.

Zara wrestled with the box. ''It's heavy,'' she said, tearing off wrapping paper.

Cleo watched her, again thinking how different their lives had become. Although while she might envy Zara her relationship with Rafe, she couldn't envy her her princess status. Cleo didn't think she could handle being a part of the royal family.

Don't think about that, she told herself. Just one more on a long list of things she couldn't think about. Like the fact that last night she'd nearly given in to Sadik, and that while he still wanted her in his bed, he had no interest in her as a person.

"This works," Zara said as she pulled the top off the large white box, then withdrew a stunning crystal bowl. The elegant piece glittered in the daylight like a massive diamond.

"Ohh, I'm going to have to borrow that one," Sabrina said, as she breezed into the gift room. "Am I too late? Did I miss the elephants?"

Zara laughed and turned to greet her half sister. "No elephants. I'm trying to convince myself there aren't going to be any."

The two women hugged, then Sabrina turned to Cleo. "I'm so glad you're back," she said, hurrying over and hugging Cleo, as well. "Your last stay was far too short. You must stay longer this time."

Cleo nodded because she couldn't speak. Her throat tightened as she stared at the two women. Both tall, slender brunettes with the same wide eyes and smiling mouths. Anyone looking at them would know they were sisters.

Sabrina took the bowl and held it up to the light. "Seriously, this is gorgeous. And I happen to know they make matching wineglasses."

Zara laughed. "I thought I'd just steal yours."

Cleo smiled, but her heart felt heavy. Obviously, in the past four months Sabrina and Zara had become close. It was bound to happen. Although they'd just met, they were in fact related by blood. They were both princesses, and Zara was marrying Sabrina's husband's second in command. They would be living in the fabled City of Thieves, several hundred miles from the Bahanian capital.

Sabrina set down the bowl, then pulled up a chair

next to Cleo and grabbed the clipboard. "I can't believe she's put you to work already. So like her."

"Hey, I torment my baby sister whenever I can." Zara winked at Cleo.

Sabrina sighed. "I wish I'd grown up with a sister. I envy you two that."

Cleo looked at Zara and Sabrina. Not only did they look alike, but they were dressed alike in expensive slacks and silk blouses. Cleo wore a loose cotton dress she should have tossed out the previous summer. "You're the sisters. I'm just someone Zara's mother took in. Not a relative at all."

Sabrina shook her head. "You're sisters in the truest sense of the word, and I'll admit to wanting to be a part of that." Her expression turned serious. "Cleo, I hope that we can all be close. I'd really like that."

While Cleo was touched by her sincerity, she also felt a little uncomfortable. "This is where I remind you I'm the only nonprincess in the group."

Sabrina playfully bumped her shoulder. "Maybe we can change that. I saw you dancing with a certain prince last night. Things looked intense."

Cleo could feel heat flaring on her cheeks. "Sorry to burst your bubble, but that's so not going to happen. I'm not in the market for an arrogant prince, no matter how handsome he might be."

"Oh. So you think he's handsome."

Cleo pressed her lips together. Trapped by her own stupid words. "He's okay."

"Uh-huh. Sure." Sabrina laughed. "Zara, we might have to do a little matchmaking with this one."

Cleo thought about how Sadik was so hot to get her

into bed now but hadn't once bothered to get in touch with her after she'd left. In four months there hadn't been a word from him.

"No matchmaking for me. Like I said, arrogant princes aren't my style."

"Too bad."

Sabrina scribbled a few notes about the bowl, then helped Zara collect the wrapping paper and throw it in a trash container at the side of the table. The bowl, along with the letter and the paperwork, went onto a display table. Zara brought over another box.

Sabrina studied the accompanying letter. "This one is from the crown prince of Lucia-Serrat. It's an island in the Indian Ocean. The crown prince of the island is a cousin of the king of Bahania." She waved a hand. "Don't ask, it's complicated. But this guy is good-looking and a widower with four sons." She glanced at Cleo. "He needs a wife."

"Too bad I'm not looking for a husband."

"You will be eventually. Although now that I think about it, I'm not sure I'd want to recommend my brothers. After all, our father was a bit of a playboy." She frowned. "He was devoted to your mother, Zara. And he loved Reyhan and Jefri's mother, at least that's what I've been told. Of course Sadik has been faithful in his own way."

Zara opened the package. Inside the box was a flat jewelry case. She opened it and caught her breath. "Can I accept this?"

She pulled out a stunning diamond necklace. Hundreds of glittering diamonds dangled, forming a vee shape. There were matching earrings and a bracelet, as well.

Sabrina touched the earrings and sighed. "Someone has fabulous taste. And, yes, you can accept it. If he's related to Dad, he's family, remember?"

Zara looked at Cleo. "At times like this I think about running for home."

"This is your home now," Cleo reminded her. Although she had to admit the necklace intimidated her, as well. But she had more important things on her mind.

"Sabrina, what did you mean about Sadik being faithful in his own way?"

Sabrina put the earrings back in the jewelry case. "Just that he's continued to mourn Kamra all these years."

Cleo was glad she was sitting down. The room tilted suddenly and her stomach began to flop over. "Kamra?"

"Sadik's fiancée." Sabrina sat back in the chair and picked up the clipboard. "They were engaged. It was an arranged match, but they seemed to get along well. She was killed in a car accident about three weeks before the wedding. Sadik took it pretty hard."

"Cleo, are you all right?" Zara asked.

Cleo forced herself to keep breathing. "Fine. So you want to keep the necklace or is it going in the discard pile?"

Her question had the desired effect. Zara was distracted. When the next box turned out to be a half-dozen camel bridles from one of the nomadic tribes, Sabrina explained that there were actual camels to go in them. That sent the two women off into a discussion as to whether camels were a better or worse gift than elephants.

Cleo tried to participate. She nodded and occasionally added a word or two. She even managed to smile. But inside, she felt numb, and just beyond the numbness was a gaping pit of intense pain and betrayal.

Sadik had loved another woman. That woman had died and now he mourned her. No wonder he only wanted Cleo in his bed. He'd already given his heart to someone else.

She'd always known there couldn't be anything serious between them, but somehow finding out that he had never been available made the situation worse. All her life she'd dreamed of being the most important person in someone's life. It was her private fantasy. And now she knew it was never going to happen with Sadik.

Until that moment she hadn't realized she had secretly hoped he would fall in love with her.

She pressed her hand to her stomach and felt hopelessness well up inside. As much as she'd thought about keeping the baby from him, she knew it wasn't possible. Not only was he likely to find out, keeping him from his child was wrong. Which meant at some point she was going to have to come clean. And then what? Would he try to take her child away from her? How could she possibly come to terms with the royal family? How could she stay in Bahania and share in the upbringing?

Everything was going wrong. She should never have come back here. Then she looked at Zara and saw the happiness on her face. This was Zara's time. Cleo couldn't ruin it. Not by refusing to show up or by running off. Somehow she would have to get through the next week. Once the wedding was over, she would have time to think and figure out what she was going to do.

Cleo escaped into the gardens. When she was outside, she finally felt as if she could breathe again. She ached inside. She supposed that a sensible person might have figured out that Sadik had loved someone else, but then a sensible person wouldn't have gotten involved with him in the first place. She felt well and truly trapped.

Worse, she still wanted him. Not just in bed, either. Even as her heart was ripped apart by the knowledge that he would never love her, she wanted to feel his arms around her.

"You need therapy," she said aloud as she crossed the garden and sank onto a bench. She breathed in the scent of the flowers and tried to find peace in the beauty all around her.

The sky was a brilliant shade of blue. The scent of the sea blended with the sweet scent of hundreds of blossoms. She touched the edge of a late-blooming rose. Her finger caught on a thorn, and she yelped as a single drop of blood formed.

"Figures," she muttered.

If only, she thought sadly. If only there was a way to change her feelings or change Sadik. But even if she was princess material, which she knew she was not, she couldn't compete with a deceased fiancée. Kamra would be ever perfect in his mind—never growing old or looking tired or snapping back. No woman could compete with a ghost.

Cleo swallowed, then suddenly surged to her feet. Her stomach rebelled against all the emotion—or maybe just against her overly large breakfast. She barely had time to bend over one of the bushes before she vomited.

In an unfortunate quirk of timing, King Hassan chose that moment to take a stroll in his garden.

She didn't know he was there until she straightened and he pressed a handkerchief in her hand.

Cleo didn't know what to do. She wanted to run but realized she was crying too hard to see. Tripping would not be a good idea. Not only would it lack a certain grace, she didn't want any harm to come to the baby.

"Come, child," the king said kindly, putting an arm around her and helping her back to the bench. "Sit and catch your breath."

Cleo allowed him to help her because her brain was too busy figuring out how she was supposed to explain throwing up in the royal garden. The king didn't look angry, but she suspected he would want an explanation.

He sat next to her and took her hand in his. "There is a royal physician on call," he said. "I will summon him."

"No!" That was the last thing she needed. "I'm fine. It's just all the excitement."

A pretty pitiful excuse but the best she could come up with under the circumstances.

Hassan studied her. He took the handkerchief and wiped her cheeks. "I see tears. I doubt they are from excitement. Tell me, Cleo. What makes you so sad?"

No way she could confess that, she thought glumly. Talking about Sadik's former fiancée would only get her in trouble.

"Is it Zara?" he asked.

"No. I mean I really miss her a lot, but she's so happy here. Plus you're her family—this is where she belongs."

The king continued to hold her hand. "Cleo, I repeat what I told you before. You are welcome to make this your home, as well. I would be delighted if you would stay in the palace. Or if you would prefer, you could live in the City of Thieves. Either way you would be close to your sister." He paused, then smiled. "I have to say that I would recommend Bahania. You do not strike me as the medieval city type."

Cleo tried to laugh but found herself crying instead. Hassan pulled her close.

"Such sadness," he murmured. "Tell me what I can do to ease your pain."

His kindness only made her cry harder. Part of her couldn't believe this was happening. Hassan wasn't just Zara's father, he was the king of Bahania. What was wrong with this picture?

Still, Cleo found comfort in his embrace. Her father had died before she was born, and she hadn't had the chance to know him at all. She'd never had a substitute father while she was growing up.

"My daughter," he said, stroking her hair. "Your troubles bring me discomfort, as well. If you do not explain what is wrong, I can not fix it."

She raised her head to gaze at him. After blinking

back the tears, she managed to speak. "You said 'my daughter.'"

"You are the beloved sister of my Zara. That makes you beloved to me, as well." He cupped her face. "You cry as if all is lost, but I know it cannot be so."

Cleo wasn't sure what weakened her resolve. Hassan's gentleness, of course, but also his willingness to claim her. She doubted he actually thought of her as a daughter, but just saying the word was enough to shatter her reticence.

"You wouldn't be nice if you knew the truth about my past," she said, in a last-ditch effort to gather some control.

"I know all I need to. You are a part of my family. As such, I want only your happiness."

She desperately wanted to believe him. Ducking her head, she grabbed back the handkerchief and sobbed into it. "I'm p-pregnant."

Hassan continued to stroke her hair. "I see. Would you like me to have the unworthy dog flogged?"

Despite her desperate situation, the visual image of Sadik hanging in chains while being beaten cheered her immensely. She risked a quick glance.

"How disappointed are you?"

The king frowned. "Why would your pregnancy disappoint me?"

Cleo flushed. "I'm not exactly a virgin."

"My claim on you as family is not conditional, my daughter. To me, you and Zara will always be perfection itself." He dropped his hand to hers. "Now tell me of the man who has left you so. I do not see an engagement ring, so he has not done the honorable thing.''

Propose? The idea was laughable. As if that would happen. Cleo sniffed. "He doesn't know. I'm going to have to tell him eventually, but first I want to figure out what I want." She smiled. "I mean, I know I want the baby, but where do I want to live and what's the best way for us to share in his or her upbringing?"

Hassan smiled. "I'm glad you want your child."

She stiffened. "Why wouldn't I? Obviously, this wasn't planned, but I will never abandon my baby. I'll do whatever I have to in order to keep us both safe." She thought of how she'd been abandoned over and over again in her life. Long ago she'd vowed that when she had children, they would know she loved them more than anything in the world.

"I see the flash of a tiger in your eyes. That bodes wells. A strong mother has strong sons."

Typical, she thought, starting to feel a little better. "I could be having a daughter."

Hassan dismissed her with a flick of his fingers. "Regardless. You must come to terms with this jackal of the desert, Cleo. I will stand beside you in whatever way I can."

While she appreciated his words, they brought her back to earth with a thump. What had she been thinking, telling Sadik's father that she was pregnant? She doubted the king would be so accommodating if he knew the truth.

"You must not mention this," she pleaded. "If people found out…" She bit her lower lip. How to convince him? "I don't want Zara's wedding spoiled by people speculating about me. She is so looking forward to the event. Please don't say anything.''

''I agree.'' He smiled. ''Your secret is safe with me, Cleo.'' He patted her hand, then rose. ''Come. You need to be in your room and resting. I will have the kitchen send you some tea to settle your stomach. You must be strong for your son.''

''Or daughter,'' she muttered as she rose, but had the feeling the king wasn't listening. She also had a very bad feeling about spilling her guts. Somehow she knew it was all going to come back and bite her in the butt. As if she didn't already have enough problems.

Twenty minutes later Cleo lay stretched out on her bed, sipping tea. The odd-smelling concoction actually made her feel better. She put the cup back on the saucer, then set both on her nightstand. Maybe a nap would make her feel better.

But before she could even close her eyes, her bedroom door burst open. Zara stormed into the room.

''You're pregnant and you didn't even tell me?''

Chapter Five

"Shouldn't you still be opening presents?" Cleo asked, knowing it was a feeble attempt at distracting Zara.

"Shouldn't you be telling me something this important?" Zara stalked to the edge of the bed and crossed her arms over her chest. "How could you keep this from me?"

Cleo could have gone head-to-head with Zara in a snit, but the hurt in her sister's eyes made her feel like slime.

"I'm sorry." She sat up and leaned against the headboard. "I guess you ran into the king."

"Yes. He came to talk to me about the presents, then managed to let it slip that you'd confessed you were pregnant. He thought I should know, which is more than you thought.''

This is what she got for trusting a man, she thought glumly. She could feel the situation spinning out of control. Who else had Hassan told, and what was going to happen if Sadik learned the truth?

She didn't want to think about that now, so she pushed those thoughts from her mind.

''You're getting married,'' Cleo began slowly. ''I wanted this time to be about you. If I'd told you, you would have gotten all worried and wanted to fix things.''

''Exactly. I care about you. I want to know what's going on in your life. Don't you think this was a big deal?''

''It is,'' Cleo admitted. ''I'm sorry.''

Zara didn't look mollified. ''So who's the father?''

''No one you know.'' Cleo shrugged and tried to look like she wasn't lying. ''After I went home, I met someone.''

Zara didn't look convinced. ''Funny how you never mentioned him in all the phone conversations we've had.''

''I didn't know if it was serious.''

''It's serious enough that you got pregnant.''

This was not going the way Cleo had hoped. ''Zara, I'm going to be fine. I don't want you to worry about me.''

''I can't help it. You're my little sister.'' Zara climbed up onto the mattress and settled next to her. ''What I don't understand is how this happened.''

Despite her concerns, Cleo couldn't help smiling.

"The usual way. I would have thought you'd figured out the facts of life by now."

Zara rolled her eyes. "You know what I mean. You've been sexually active for a long time. How come you got pregnant this time?"

"Bad timing," Cleo admitted. "I'd gone off the pill to give my body a rest. I wasn't expecting to get involved with someone so I wasn't prepared."

Zara looked stunned. "You had unprotected sex?"

"We used a condom, but things happen."

Actually what had happened was that one night she and Sadik had been so hot for each other, they'd both forgotten birth control. She hadn't even realized it until several days later, when she'd been on her way home. They had been irresponsible, and now she was paying the price.

"I can't believe this," Zara breathed.

"Tell me about it." Cleo looked at her sister. "I know you're upset. This is exactly why I didn't want you to know. The thing is, Zara, I'll be fine, as will my baby. This is your time. You have a beautiful wedding in a week. I don't want you thinking about anything else. Can't we forget this and deal with it after you get back from your honeymoon?"

"I didn't think you were still going to be here then."

Cleo didn't know what was going to happen, now that the news was out. "We can deal with it either together or long-distance. I promise."

Slowly Zara nodded. "I'm giving in because I don't have a choice. You're a grown-up. You have to be responsible for your own life. I just wish you had told me."

"I'm sorry," Cleo repeated, thinking that she had a few wishes of her own.

The difference between a formal state dinner and an informal state dinner was usually found in the size and the details.

Cleo paused at the entrance to the cocktail party and studied the room. Flowers bloomed everywhere—providing a sweet scent and creating the sense of being in a garden. Small white lights twinkled, candles flickered and an immense crowd of people circulated and talked. The informal dinner had been for about two hundred people. There had to be at least five times that number in attendance to honor the bride and groom. Everyone glittered and sparkled, leaving her feeling like a very out-of-place, country cousin. A very tired country cousin.

She hadn't slept in two days. Not since she'd found out that the king had told Zara about her pregnancy. So far no one else seemed to know, so she was keeping her fingers crossed that she could escape the situation without too much trouble.

A waiter paused and offered her a glass of champagne. Cleo declined, then decided to head to the bar where she could get her club soda with lime and pass it off as a cocktail. At least she felt reasonably attractive. Her red, beaded gown skimmed over her curves in such a way as to make her feel like a pinup girl from the 1940s. A twist of fabric in the midsection hid her tummy, which was good because it had really started sticking out. She was approaching her fifth month and none of her regular pants would fit. She was going to have to hit the maternity stores before long. But that trip would have to wait until she headed home.

The good news was she hadn't thrown up in the past couple of days. Maybe that cookie toss into the royal garden had been her last.

Less than ten feet from the bar, she came to a dead stop. Sadik stood across the room, and the second she saw him, she knew that he'd been told about the baby. His dark gaze fell immediately to her midsection and the look of accusation on his face rooted her to the floor. Even when he headed toward her, tall, angry and determined, she couldn't seem to make herself run.

He grabbed her arm and herded her toward the far end of the room where there weren't so many people. She glanced around to see if she could find someone to rescue her, then figured there was no point in putting off the inevitable.

Think fast, she told herself. She had to come up with a plausible story. She'd tell him what she told Zara— that she'd met someone. After all, she'd already hinted there was another man in her past. She needed to buy herself time. If she told him it was his baby, he would take over her life and she would lose the ability to make decisions. It's not that she wanted to keep Sadik from his child; she wanted to make sure he didn't ace her out of the picture.

He led her into a small alcove, then positioned her so her back was to the main room, but he faced that direction. Probably so he could make sure they weren't interrupted or overheard.

"Is it true?" he asked by way of a greeting. "Are you pregnant?"

She reminded herself that the king had not only called the father of her child a jackal of the desert but had offered to have him flogged. She wondered if Hassan would be willing to go through with the latter if he found out the father in question was his own son.

Once again the idea of Sadik in chains gave her comfort, however small. She laced her fingers together in front of her waist and squeezed her palms together.

"I am pregnant," she said slowly, "but before you get all hot and possessive, I want to make it clear that it's not your baby. I've already told you, there's someone else in my life now. The child is his."

Dark eyes narrowed slightly. Sadik seemed to see into her soul. Then he shook his head in a dismissal that made her heart sink.

"The child is mine. You could not be with another man after being with me."

His flat statement made her want to scream. Worse, it was true, and if she tried to deny it too hard, he was going to see right through her. Panic threatened.

Sadik took hold of her upper arms and pulled her close. As much as she wanted to look away, he compelled her to meet his gaze. His expression turned cold and more than a little scary.

"Make no mistake," he said softly, menace in every syllable. "Bahanian law will not allow a royal child to be taken out of the country without the king's permission. However much my father might claim you as his daughter, he will not turn his back on his first grandson. If you do not admit the truth to me now, I will go to my father and tell him of our relationship. I will explain that I believe the child to be mine and insist you be examined by a doctor. If you are more than four months along…"

He stopped talking, but there was no point in finishing the threat. Cleo wasn't an idiot. She knew that the king's favor couldn't be stretched very far. Hassan wouldn't let her take away his grandchild, and Sadik would do everything he promised.

He continued to stare at her face. "Tell me again, Cleo. Tell me the child is not mine."

She waited as long as she could, then exhaled the truth. "I can't."

His self-satisfied smile tore at her heart. Her first thought was to run. If she went fast enough and far enough they could never find her. But before she could even take a step, Sadik was shaking his head. His smile faded.

"Do not think you can escape me. We are talking about my son. My heir."

"So if I have a girl, I'm free to go," she said bitterly, hating that his words had ripped her apart. She didn't simply fear his threats, she felt as if he'd destroyed every hint of a dream. Sadik didn't care about her—he never had. As far as he was concerned, she was little more than a vessel. She was the carrier of his offspring, and not a person in her own right.

"I am Prince Sadik of Bahania. I will have a son."

That almost made her smile. "As long as you had that conversation with your sperm, Sadik. You did realize those little guys might have a mind of their own, right?"

He frowned, as if mothers of royal babies didn't discuss such things.

She jerked free of his hold and walked to the far end of the alcove. Even as she placed her hands against the cool walls, she knew there was no escape. Not from him and not from her circumstances.

Her eyes burned, and her throat tightened, but her pain was too deep for tears. Sadness tugged at her, making it difficult to stay standing.

"What happens now?" she asked, barely able to form the words, then changed her mind. "Don't bother. I know what happens. You keep a close watch on me until the child is born, but then what?" She swallowed, not wanting to hear the truth but desperate to know. "How long until you throw me out of the palace?"

He was at her side in an instant. He grabbed her and turned her toward him. Rage tightened his face. She hadn't known he was capable of such emotion and it should have frightened her, but she had other things to worry about. Once she knew his plans, she could come up with her own ideas of how to escape, either before or after the child was born. Because no matter how he threatened her, she would never abandon her child.

"Is that what you think?" he demanded. "That I would cast you into the streets?"

"You don't care about me. Until now you only wanted me to warm your bed. Now that you know I'm pregnant, you'll want me to carry the baby to term, but after that I'll be of no use to you."

He released her as if she'd burned him. Sadik stalked to the entrance of the alcove and turned back to face her.

"You think so little of me," he said.

"I'm a realist. All I want to know are your plans."

"You will be the mother of my son. As such, you are to be honored."

Her racing heart slowed slightly. "You wouldn't expect me to leave my child and just disappear?"

"I am not an animal."

She wasn't sure she believed him, but his words gave her hope. If he was willing to say that, then maybe she could go to the king for assurances. The idea of making some kind of coparenting plan work seemed impossible, but she would do anything to stay with her baby.

He glared at her. "I see the doubt in your eyes. How is that possible? In what way have I so betrayed you that you would not trust me now?"

"How much time do you have?" she asked, not caring that she continued to stir his temper. In truth she wanted him to—

The sudden sensation of butterflies in her stomach surprised her into silence. She wasn't nervous...she was furious that she'd been put into this situation, and relieved that at least for now she didn't have to worry about losing her child. There was no reason she should be feeling a fluttering sensation.

Cleo's breath caught. Sadik was at her side in a second, putting his arm around her to support her weight. "What is wrong? Do you need to sit down? Should I call a doctor?"

He was so solicitous and obviously worried that she nearly laughed out loud. Then she remembered that none of his attentions were about her.

"I'm fine," she said, as the fluttering continued. "I just felt the baby move."

He frowned. "Is that good? Are you supposed to?"

She considered him the enemy in this situation. Worse, she had feelings for him she wasn't willing to explore or define. The man tempted her beyond reason and made her forget herself. The safest course of action would be to get as far away as possible. But he was also the father of her child. While growing up she'd seen countless fathers who wanted nothing to do with their offspring. At least Sadik showed interest.

So against her better judgment, she took his hand in hers and brought it to her belly, where the fluttering was the strongest. She pressed his fingers into her belly.

"Can you feel that?" she asked in a whisper. "It's the first time I've felt the baby move."

He was still, then his fingers moved slightly and he grinned at her. "My son is strong."

She pushed his hands away and rolled her eyes. "You make me crazy."

He ignored that and stared at her stomach. "You do not seem very large in the belly."

"I'm not showing a lot right now," she agreed. "I'm a week into my fifth month so I would imagine I'm going to pop anytime now."

"Pop?"

"Get huge. I'm too short to carry the baby with any grace and style. Tall women can hide their pregnancy longer."

"Why would you want to hide such a blessing?"

For one thing she hadn't wanted him to know. For another… She drew in a breath. "Sadik, you have to promise me something. We can't let everyone know about this. Not until after Zara's wedding. I don't want her big day spoiled by speculation."

Sadik considered her words, then nodded. "I agree that the happiness of my sister must come first. In return for this, I want your word that you won't steal away after the wedding."

She hadn't considered ducking out but realized the thought would have occurred to her eventually. "I promise," she said.

"Good." He put his arm around her. "We have much to discuss. I wish to know everything you've experienced with the child and I will share in the changes as they occur."

She thought of how she'd had morning sickness just about twenty-four hours a day and how *her* body was the one that was going to swell like a watermelon. "I don't think there's going to be a whole lot of sharing," she said glumly. "I can tell you what I've experienced, but that's not the same."

"I have many questions," he said as if she hadn't spoken. "When did you first realize you were pregnant? Have you been eating right? Why did you not tell me?"

Weariness descended. Cleo told herself that she should be grateful that Sadik wasn't furious with her anymore. She was even surprised that he was taking it so well. But there were so many things she didn't understand and situations she wasn't willing to deal with at the moment.

She slipped away from his embrace. Everything was different now. He saw her as the mother of his child, so it was unlikely he would want her in his bed. The thought should have made her relieved, but instead she felt sad.

"I'm really tired," she said. "Would you mind if we tabled the discussion until later?"

He hesitated, then nodded his agreement. "Would you like me to get you something to drink?"

"Yes, please."

She wasn't all that thirsty, but she did need some time alone. Her composure had scattered and she had to collect herself before the formal dinner.

Sadik headed for the bar, but his mind was not on his task. A baby. When his father had mentioned Cleo was pregnant, Sadik had known right away that the child had to be his. He'd felt delighted by the news.

Now that he had confirmation, elation welled up inside of him. He wanted to announce the news to the world. Still, he would keep the secret until after Zara's wedding. Cleo's concern for her sister was well-founded.

How long had he longed for a son? After Kamra's death, he had put aside his plans for a family. He'd known that eventually he would have to marry and have children, but he'd had no desire to hurry the process. This unexpected bounty made him pleased with the world.

He requested the club soda and lime, then headed back to where he'd left Cleo. He could see her sitting on a chair by the wall. She looked stunned—as if their encounter had drained her. She needed her rest, he decided. He would make sure she was in bed early that evening. She needed her strength so that his son would grow and develop inside of her.

They were bound now, he thought. Cleo would always be the mother of his son. The concept should have discomfited him, yet it did not. She had many fine qualities to pass on to their child. She continued to challenge and defy him, even now. He would very much enjoy the process of taming her.

"I can't believe this is happening," Zara said as the carriage moved forward. She perched uneasily on the edge of the cushioned seat in the open conveyance, her flowers gripped tightly in her hand.

Cleo sat opposite and tried not to mind that she was facing the wrong direction. As the bride, it was right that Zara should face forward. Under normal circumstances, she wouldn't mind. However, while her morning sickness seemed to have disappeared, her stomach often felt faintly unsettled, leaving Cleo concerned that the tossing-her-cookies portion of her pregnancy might make an unexpected return.

"Just smile and wave," Cleo said, glancing at the crowd lining either side of the road.

Their open, horse-drawn carriage moved slowly, accompanied by cheers and whistles from those who had come out to watch. Mounted guards rode next to them, as much to be part of the spectacle as to offer protection. Cleo figured it was unlikely that anyone was about to kidnap the king's daughter.

"I don't think I can do this," Zara said softly, her face pale, her eyes wide.

"You'll be fine." Cleo motioned to her dress. "I don't think you can return that."

Zara laughed, then smoothed the front of her designer creation. The long-sleeved wedding gown looked like something out of a fairy tale. Hand-sewn beads caught the sunlight. Yards and yards of silk and lace cascaded to the ground. With her hair upswept and anchored by an antique tiara, Zara was truly a royal princess.

Cleo figured even *she* didn't look half-bad. Her rose-colored gown had been cut low and fell straight from below her bodice. The empire style concealed her stomach, which seemed to have suddenly puffed out in the past couple of days. Zara wore diamonds at her ears and around her throat, while Cleo had been accessorized with pearls. Diamond and pearl earrings glittered on her lobes. A stunning circle of pearls, decorated with a diamond enhancer, draped down to the curve of her breasts.

"I'm going to throw up," Zara announced.

"You're going to be fine. Keep smiling and waving. It's not a big job, especially for someone with all your education."

Zara laughed again. "Okay. You're distracting me. I like that."

Cleo switched her cascade of flowers to her other hand. "I'm having second thoughts about refusing the tiara. Do you think I should have worn it?"

Zara glanced at her spiky hair. "Could we have anchored it?"

They had a detailed conversation about the pros and cons of hair accessories, then Cleo switched the conversation to shoes. They pulled up in front of the church before Zara had a chance to realize where they were.

A uniformed guard approached their carriage. King Hassan had ridden with the groom in a carriage in front of theirs. The princes shared the one behind Zara's, with Sabrina and her husband bringing up the rear.

The small door was opened and Cleo rose to exit first assisted by the waiting footmen. She managed to get down the two steps without falling. Although she didn't actually look for Sadik, she was aware of him. The man watched her constantly. She tried to take comfort in his attention, but knew that it had nothing to do with her and everything to do with the baby.

Don't go there now, she told herself. This day was about Zara.

Her sister managed to get out of the carriage without a mishap. Sabrina joined them, urging them into the church. At the top of the stairs leading into the building, they turned and waved to the waiting crowd. A cheer rose.

"Keep breathing," Sabrina said as they stepped into the cool darkness of the foyer.

Sabrina's husband had already escorted the groom and the princes up the aisle. The organ music changed, cueing the women that it was time.

Sabrina stood in front, with Cleo to follow. Hassan stopped and kissed his daughter, then stepped next to Cleo.

"You are beauty personified," he murmured, touching his lips to her cheek. "I am most proud."

Cleo wondered if he was talking about the baby. As far as she could tell, the king still didn't know that Sadik was the father, but maybe his son had told him the truth. Either way, this wasn't the time for a lengthy conversation.

She gave Hassan a smile. He squeezed her hand, then moved behind her to stand next to Zara.

The twenty-foot double wooden doors opened, revealing the crowded church and the long center aisle. Cleo's stomach clenched.

Sabrina turned around and winked. "Show time," she said in a stage whisper. "If you get nervous, picture everyone naked."

Chapter Six

Cleo hadn't thought the actual wedding through. She'd seen the stacks and stacks of replies from every corner of the globe. She'd seen the gift rooms and had attended the rehearsal in the massive church. But nothing had prepared her for the vast space to be crammed full of members of the extended royal family, visiting dignitaries, family friends and a couple of thousand guests.

Organ music soared to the arched ceiling of the fourteenth-century church. Saints watched from stained-glass windows, their hands outstretched.

Cleo found herself shaking with unexpected nerves. The only thing that kept her going was watching Sabrina ahead of her. Zara's half sister moved slowly, in time with the music. Cleo kept her pace even as she struggled to not turn and run.

She could hear the faint murmurings of the guests as they watched her. At least her bouquet of flowers cascaded down to her knees, hiding her bulging belly. She didn't want there to be any speculation—not on Zara's day.

As she approached the front of the church, she saw Rafe. He grinned at her, then looked past her as the organ music shifted to the wedding march. Everyone stood. Cleo wanted to turn around and watch her sister, but she still had about ten feet to go. Her gaze lingered on Rafe, and she watched his expression change to one of love and wonder. He looked as if he'd been waiting for Zara all his life.

Perhaps he had, Cleo thought as she stepped into place next to Sabrina. Perhaps she was his one true love.

Cleo casually glanced at Sadik, who stood behind Prince Kardal, who was Sabrina's husband. Sadik didn't seem to care that the bride had entered the church. He stared at Cleo as if he could claim her with a look.

She fought against a feeling of sadness. Possession was not love, and whatever feelings he had for her were just about the baby. Intense longing filled her—longing for what Zara had. A family, a man who loved her more than anyone in the world, a place to belong. Was it so wrong to want to be a part of something? She'd spent her whole life on the fringes, always on the outside looking in. She had a bad feeling that wasn't going to change.

Cleo shook off her unhappy thoughts and turned her attention to her sister. Zara looked like a princess as she walked up the aisle, her father escorting her. Everything about the moment was perfect, and no more than Zara deserved.

Kissing the bride was not a part of the Bahania ceremony, but Rafe did it, anyway. Cleo joined in the spontaneous applause as the couple clung to each other before turning and facing their happy guests. Bells rang, the vibrant sound echoing in the church.

The bride and groom started down the aisle. Cleo went next, expecting to link arms with Kardal, but he had shifted positions with Sadik, and she found herself close to the one man who could—despite everything— still take her breath away.

"You are radiance itself," he murmured as they strolled down the aisle. He nodded at several guests. No doubt rulers of distant lands and personal friends of the family.

"Thank you."

As they had on the way up, the crowd continued to overwhelm her. This was for real, she thought, stunned and amazed. Her foster sister, the same person she'd fought with about bathroom time and who had once tried to pierce her ears with a sewing needle was an honest-to-goodness princess married to a sheik.

Even more shattering she, Cleo, was walking down the aisle of an eight-hundred-year-old church, next to a prince who could trace his bloodline back a thousand years. Oh, and she was pregnant by him.

Her head spun when they stepped outside and she

saw that thousands had gathered around the church. In a special area set up to the left of the church, several dozen television crews reported on the event for the international news. Still cameras flashed, taking pictures everywhere.

The horse-drawn carriages stood waiting. After Rafe and Zara moved off in theirs, Sadik helped her into the next one. Thank goodness Kardal and Sabrina sat with them. Cleo didn't think she was capable of forming words let alone dealing with Sadik right now.

"You look shell-shocked," Sabrina said kindly as their carriage started forward. "I'm not surprised. This is a little overwhelming for me and I've been through it before."

Cleo nodded, afraid that if she tried to speak she would either scream or cry. Neither would be especially helpful.

They returned to the palace. Pictures were taken, then the royal family joined the reception already in progress.

The largest palace ballroom had been transformed into fairyland, Cleo thought, still dazed. Thousands of yards of beaded tulle decorated the walls and pillars. Lights twinkled beside a cascading waterfall that hadn't been there just a few days before. Buffets had been set up against three walls, and there seemed to be enough food to take care of several nations at once. A large orchestra played continuously. Champagne fountains flowed at both ends of the head table where Cleo found she had been seated next to Sadik. His doing, no doubt.

She managed to go through the motions, toasting her sister, offering best wishes, meeting people. Sadik

stayed at her side for much of the afternoon. When
Rafe and Zara disappeared to change for their honeymoon, he swept her into his arms and danced with her.

"I think they will enjoy their time away," he said,
speaking quietly into her ear.

"Yes. They will." Her mouth felt numb. She knew
she was talking, but she couldn't feel her lips moving.

The king had arranged for the newlyweds to spend
several weeks on his private yacht. They would cruise
through the Mediterranean, then up the coast of Spain
to France and England.

Her gaze swept over the room and something inside
of her snapped. This wasn't her world; she didn't belong here. Nothing about the situation felt right.

But even as she prepared to run, she felt a fluttering
sensation in her belly. Her baby turned or kicked, or
maybe just waved. It was enough to remind her that
there was more at stake than her own desire to belong.
If she left, she would have to abandon her child, and
Cleo was willing to walk through hell before ever doing that.

Yet compromise seemed hopeless. How were she
and Sadik supposed to come to terms? Obviously, she
would have to live in Bahania, but how? She refused
to be supported, assuming that was what he had in
mind. Yet who was going to give the former mistress
of a royal prince any kind of job?

Sadik watched the light fade from Cleo's blue eyes.
She had begun the morning bursting with happiness for
her sister, but somehow over the past few hours it had
slowly disappeared until she looked wounded.

He did not like to think of her so, and tried to shake off the image. Still, there was no energy in her speech, and she only picked at her food.

Rafe and Zara waved to their guests and ducked out the far door. Sadik took advantage of the distraction and quickly ushered Cleo toward a side exit that led to the private wing of the palace.

"Where are we going?" she demanded, showing spirit for the first time that afternoon.

"I think we have things to discuss."

"Oh, sure. *Now* you want to talk. Isn't that just like a man. Before, when I had things to say, you weren't interested. You were all caught up in finding out about the baby. Well maybe I don't want to talk to you."

Sadik ignored her outburst, just as he ignored the way she tugged on his hand as if trying to escape.

"There is no point," he said calmly, continuing to lead the way. "I have no plans to release you."

"That's my big fear."

When they reached the double doors leading into his private quarters, he slowed to study her. Cleo stared at the doors as if they led to a prison.

He smiled. "I promise I will not have you tortured once you step inside."

"It's not the torture I'm afraid of."

Was she remembering, as he was, what had happened the last time they had been in these rooms together? Passion had exploded between them until they'd had no choice but to give in. They'd made love endlessly, every chance they had, clinging to each other, touching, taking, offering. He'd never known such desire.

He opened the door, then stepped back to allow her to go first. Cleo entered cautiously, glancing around as if checking to see all was as she remembered.

"Nothing has changed," he told her.

"If you're talking about the furniture, I guess you're right. If you mean everything else, you couldn't be more wrong."

She crossed the large living room to the French doors that led to the common balcony. From there it was a relatively short walk back to her own suite. But she didn't try to escape. Instead she simply pressed her fingers against the glass.

"This is how birds must feel," she said quietly. "They can see to the other side, but something invisible prevents them from flying away."

He frowned. "Of what do you speak?"

She sighed. "Nothing. Everything. The wedding went very well."

The change of topic confused him. "I'm sure Zara and Rafe will be very happy."

She nodded but didn't say more. Drawn by a certainty that something was very wrong, he crossed to stand behind her. "What troubles you?"

She shook her head. He saw a single tear slide down her cheek.

Had she defied him, he could have fought her on equal terms and been confident in his victory. But fragility baffled him—especially in Cleo. She was the most tempting woman he'd ever met, and while her beauty kept him enthralled, he found her willingness to fearlessly clash with him one of her most intriguing features.

"What pains you so?"

"You wouldn't understand."

"I am an intelligent, successful man who knows much of the world. I am sure I could follow along."

She looked at him. Tears glittered in her large, blue eyes. She swallowed. "All those months, you never tried to get in touch with me. I doubt you even thought of me. Then the second you found out I'm pregnant, you suddenly act as if you own me. I'm trapped like a bird in a cage. I can't leave and take my child, and I won't abandon my baby. So here I am. No choices, no life, save that of being the vessel for your child. It's not exactly the future I had envisioned for myself."

He didn't know which comment to address first, then went with the one he most understood.

"You left my bed."

She stared at him. "What does that have to do with anything?"

"I did not ask you to leave—you simply chose to go away."

"We've been over this material before. Yes, I left before you asked me to. I'm sure you were heartbroken for a nanosecond. So what?"

"Why would I reward such inappropriate behavior by contacting you?"

"I am not your wayward teenager. You have no right to find my behavior wanting and then punish me for it." She glared at him as if he were the most stupid man on earth. "Well?"

Sadik would not have admitted it, even under torture, but he didn't know what to say to her. Of course he hadn't gotten in touch with her. For one thing he'd known that she was returning for her sister's wedding. For another, *she had left him.* No matter how much he explained the gravity of her disobedience, she refused to understand. He had wanted her in his bed. It was a great honor to be desired by him. He had lavished her with attention and had tried to do the same with gifts, and she had walked out. He resented her ability to simply turn her back on him.

Not that he'd missed her, he reminded himself, refusing to acknowledge the emptiness he'd felt when she disappeared from his life. He had barely thought of her at all.

"You are not a trapped bird," he said, trying a different tack. "As the mother of my son, you will be revered."

She rolled her eyes, then turned her attention back to the view of the ocean beyond the glass doors. "You're impossible. I don't know why I'm even bothering to have this conversation."

Sadik would never get it, Cleo thought. And she couldn't explain without confessing things she didn't want to say. He'd made it more than clear that he resented her having the strength of will to leave him before he was ready to have her go, but he'd never admitted to even one tender feeling. If he'd said he *liked* her, that would help.

"What are you thinking?" he asked, coming up behind her and placing his hands on her shoulders.

"That I want to go home."

"This is your home now."

That's what she was afraid of.

She stared unseeingly at the ocean, wishing she

could stow away on Zara's honeymoon yacht, then make her escape in Spain. Although without money or a passport she wouldn't get far. If she'd thought this through, she would have made alternative plans for her—

A warm, soft pressure on her bare shoulder caught her attention. Cleo's breath stalled in her throat as Sadik bent lower and kissed her skin again. As her dress wasn't loose enough for him to simply pull it off her shoulders, she had to guess that while she'd been deep in thought, he'd been unfastening her zipper. Geez— and she hadn't even noticed!

He tilted his head and moved closer, nibbling on the side of her neck. Shivers made her break out in goose bumps while liquid desire poured through her.

Just for a second she promised herself as her eyes closed. She would only give in for a little bit and then she would pull away and tell him this was a mistake. After all, Sadik was four hundred kinds of wrong for her, and making love with him would only complicate the situation.

It's not as if he can get you pregnant.

The small voice in her head made a lot of sense, she thought hazily as his hot breath caressed her. He kissed across the back of her neck—soft, teasing kisses that made it nearly impossible to stay standing. She and Sadik might come from different worlds and have completely different views of things, but they sure got along in bed.

Don't think about that, she told herself. She had to stay in control. While it was true that she couldn't get any more pregnant than she was, there were other ramifications if they made love. What about the state of her heart? Wasn't she at risk? Isn't that the reason she'd run home in the first place?

"You think too much," Sadik complained as he turned her in his arms and pulled her close. "I can hear the chatter. Stop thinking. Only feel."

Before she could work up an indignant reply, he kissed her mouth.

The sensation was both tempting and familiar. So familiar, she thought with a sigh. His strong arms encircled her body, allowing her the illusions of being both delicate and petite. He held her with a combination of passion and possession that should have annoyed her but only made her want him more.

He didn't deepen their kiss. Not at first. Instead he teased her with light pressure and tiny nibbles. He sucked on her lower lip, then finally, when she couldn't stand it anymore, brushed her tongue with his.

Fire shot through her. Against her will Cleo wrapped her arms around him. She felt his strength, the broadness of his back. He was tall and every inch a male. Already she was damp and swelling as her body prepared itself for him. She wanted him to touch her everywhere. She wanted him inside of her. She needed to make love with him with a desperation that left her both breathless and afraid.

When he broke the kiss, she moaned a protest. He laughed. "Come, my goddess. I will not make you wait long. But I think we would do better on my bed."

He took her hand and led her toward the bedroom she remembered so well. It was large and filled with masculine oversize furniture. She remembered teasing him about the size of his bed and the dresser. He could have parties for large groups on the former. She'd been joking, but he'd taken her words seriously.

"No one could touch you," he'd growled, claiming her with a kiss. She was his alone. His to desire, his to take, his to pleasure.

Cleo remembered how much she'd wanted the words to be true for more than an afternoon. But they hadn't been. And nothing had changed.

Maybe this was a mistake.

She turned to the prince. "Sadik, I don't think we should do this."

"We must," he said simply, and reached for the necklace clasp at the base of her neck.

When he'd removed her jewelry, he had her sit in a chair in the corner. Gently, nearly reverently, he removed her shoes. When her open-toed, high-heeled sandals hit the floor, she started to rise. Maybe to help him or maybe to run. She wasn't sure. But she didn't get the opportunity.

Sadik put a restraining hand on her arm. "Not yet." Then he raised her dress to her thighs and bent down to kiss the inside of her knees.

Even as his lips pressed against her skin, he moved his hands up and down her legs. His long fingers touched every inch of her calves, before moving higher and stroking her thighs. As he caressed her and reduced her to a melting shell of desire, he spoke of his pleasure in her body.

"So rich and lush," he murmured, licking the inside of her thigh and making her squirm. "Your scent intoxicates me, Cleo. So far I do not see any changes, but I know they are there. The thought of your body growing big with my son excites me.''

She was torn between wanting to be with him and knowing it was a big mistake. What tipped the scale was the knowledge that he wasn't going to be one of those men who found a pregnant woman as unsexy as a cow. Cleo had spent her entire life insecure about her short body and womanly curves. Somehow she'd never felt as if everything went together. Even though she'd had plenty of male attention, it hadn't been the right kind. But Sadik's words always seemed to hit her where she lived. She believed he genuinely adored every inch of her—pregnant or not. He made her feel irresistible, and that combined with her need for him made him irresistible, as well.

He straightened and slipped off his jacket, then loosened his tie and his cuffs. Without saying a word, he rose, then helped her to her feet. They crossed to the bed, where he finished unzipping her dress. The rose-colored garment fell to the floor.

Sadik gazed at her breasts, which had become enlarged in the past couple of months, then at her swelling belly. She'd felt unattractive and awkward right up until he smiled in delight and gathered her close.

He kissed her with a reverence that broke through her defenses and left her wanting and vulnerable. Her arms came up of their own accord. She clung to him, needing to feel him pressing against her. She knew that he was already aroused, but the feel of his hardness reassured her and fueled her body's passion.

He cupped her face in his hands and kissed her cheeks, her eyelids, her nose and her chin. He licked the hollow of her throat, then journeyed lower to the edge of her bra where he lightly teased the exposed curves.

Sadik had been right when he'd said she couldn't possibly be with another man after being with him. As he touched her, she found herself remembering what it had been like when they'd been together before. She couldn't imagine ever wanting anyone else, no matter how long she lived.

He reached behind her and unfastened her bra. As if he knew her breasts were tender, he cupped her curves as the bra slipped down. He gently rubbed his lips against her tight nipples, not pressing at all, just teasing until they grew more rigid and heat seemed to flare from every inch of her skin.

"So beautiful," he breathed.

She thought about pointing out that the veins seemed more prominent than the last time he'd seen her chest and that her skin flushed more easily. She could have done twenty minutes on how she was ambivalent about her growing belly—both appreciating that she was carrying a healthy child and hating that she was getting fatter by the day.

But when he licked her right nipple, all rational thought fled. What did body image matter when one could be in the arms of a man who knew how to make her feel incredible?

He helped her onto the bed and settled next to her. Somewhere along the way he had discarded his shoes and socks, along with his dress shirt. As Cleo brushed her hand against his bare chest, he stroked her arms, then lightly traced the hollow between her breasts.

"I see many changes," he said softly, and kissed her mouth. "You have grown even more beautiful. I can't wait to see you big and round. You will leave grown men weeping with desire."

She smiled. "I can't wait for that, either. Seeing as I've never had a grown man weep with desire, I figure I'm due."

He moved his hand down to the swell of her belly. "You are the most perfect woman. So many curves. Your flesh yields to me with a softness designed to please a man."

At barely two inches over five feet, Cleo had battled with her weight all her life. Those last fifteen pounds constantly crept up on her, and she had to struggle for weeks to get them off. Sadik had seen her at the high end of her weight cycle. After ten minutes of his verbal worship, she'd been ready to toss out her Diet Delight food scale forever.

He placed his hand on her stomach. Pride darkened his eyes.

She knew he'd gone all male and "this is my son," but before she could slap his arm away or remind him the baby might be a girl, he moved lower.

Her hips immediately pulsed in anticipation. Sadik helped her off with her panties, then slowly slipped his fingers between her thighs.

She was already slick with wanting. He smiled when he encountered damp curls and the swollen flesh beyond.

"Always ready," he murmured, and kissed her belly. "Your desire makes me want to forget myself, but then I would miss pleasing you."

He shifted slightly and licked her breasts. As his tongue stroked one sensitive nipple, his fingers sought and found her point of greatest sensitivity. He explored the small knot of nerves, rubbing lightly, circling, slipping away and then returning.

It had been so long, Cleo thought, as intense feelings filled her. Somehow, from the first, he'd known the exact rhythm to bring her to the edge in about forty seconds. Even as his thumb stroked, his middle finger slipped inside and pushed up. She felt her body contract.

Not yet, she thought frantically, trying to disconnect from what they were doing. It was too soon. She hated the power he had over her, even as she began to surrender.

He continued to touch her. Her body was on fire, and with every moment of contact, the flames licked higher. If he would just stop sucking on her breast, or take his finger out of her, she might have a shot at control. If he would just—

Surrender caught her unaware. Her body tensed, and without warning the tremors began. Her breath caught as she went rigid, then relaxed completely as he moved lightly against her trembling flesh, urging her on and drawing out every last drop of pleasure.

When she had finally returned to sanity, he moved down on the bed.

"Sadik, I'm more than content," she murmured. "Really, you don't have to do any more."

"Perhaps I want to."

She knew what he would do next and parted her

thighs. As he knelt between her legs, she drew up her knees and dug her heels into the mattress.

The first time he'd insisted on this most intimate kiss after he'd already brought her to climax, she'd flat-out told him he was crazy. She was done. It had been great, but her time at the party was over.

He had managed to convince her otherwise.

Now he lowered his head and licked her. She was exquisitely sensitive and the feel of his tongue on her nearly brought her up into a sitting position. Heat flooded her, making her want to beg him to hurry, even as she needed the experience to go on for as long as possible.

He carried her higher and higher, and when she was close to exploding, he gently put a finger inside of her.

The back and forth movement mimicked the act to follow. He used both his mouth and his finger, first one and then two, until she was on the verge of climaxing. Then he used only his finger until the tension subsided.

Over and over he repeated the process until finally she felt herself falling. Slow, rolling releases surged through her body. They were like the tide, rushing in, one after the other, then slowly withdrawing. The lower intensity meant she could continue indefinitely and he drew the surreal experience on for several minutes.

When it became impossible for her to catch her breath, he stopped long enough to remove his trousers and briefs. Then he knelt between her legs and entered her.

At the first whisper of contact, she began to climax again. He pushed in, filling her, making her cling to him. They gazed into each other's eyes, connecting in the most intimate way possible. With each thrust he pushed her over the edge.

She tried to hold back, to stop and gain some control, but it was impossible. Being with him had always made her surrender.

He moved slowly, making them both wait. She finally knew that she couldn't hold on any longer.

She tightened her muscles as hard as she could and tilted her hips. The unexpected action made him stiffen, then he called out her name, his voice hoarse. One more quick thrust and his body shuddered inside of her. Her own muscles contracted around him in a final release, sucking the last of her strength. She lay on the bed unable to move, barely able to breathe, sated beyond all reasonable expectation.

"I'd forgotten you were this good in bed," she managed to say.

Sadik chuckled. "No, my goddess. You had not forgotten a thing."

Of course he was telling the truth, but two could play at that game. "Had you?"

His smiled faded. "No. Not even when I tried."

Chapter Seven

Okay, so the fact that he hadn't forgotten about how good they were in bed meant what? Cleo tried to figure out if there were any nuances to his words, or if she should respond in some way. But before she could come up with a strategy, Sadik bent low and kissed her breasts.

"The color of your nipples has changed," he said.

Cleo half raised herself to look. "Really?"

"You have not noticed?"

She couldn't help smiling. "I have to admit I don't spend a lot of my day looking at myself naked."

Sadik brushed her belly with his hand. "I would spend all day gazing at you naked, if it were possible."

The postlovemaking glow left her vulnerable. She didn't think this was a good time to be listening to his compliments. They would only get her in trouble. The true disaster would be if she actually started to believe they meant something.

He nuzzled her belly. "And here, you have a dark line forming." He placed his hands on either side of her stomach. "You carry my son."

She stretched back on the bed. "The baby could be a girl. You might want to consider that."

He ignored her…like *that* was a surprise. "My son. The first male grandchild of the king of Bahania."

"I'm done arguing about the baby's gender," she told him. "Just be prepared to be wrong."

His self-satisfied smile made her want to cuff him. "I am never wrong."

She started to respond but was distracted by fluttering in her belly. "It's happening," she said, knowing she was crazy for wanting to share this with him.

But the baby's tiny signs of life were precious to her, and there was no one else on the planet who would care as much, except for Sadik.

"Show me," he demanded.

She took his hands and shifted them to the side. He pressed in slightly, then grinned when he felt the vibration.

"He is strong."

"Apparently."

Sadik was still as the movements continued. His hands were warm and comforting. As she watched, his expression tightened. His eyes darkened with emotion. It took her a couple of seconds to figure out he felt love for their unborn child. Love and adoration.

On the one hand Cleo knew she should be happy

that he was so accepting of the baby's presence. He could have been annoyed or denied that it was his. Then she reminded herself that if he were to have denied the child, she would have been free to leave. So that would have been a good thing.

Or would it? Perversely, she was *glad* he wanted their baby, even though it completely messed up her life. She hadn't allowed herself to think through all the ramifications of having to live here. She had no idea what she was going to do with herself or what her role would be.

Now, seeing how much Sadik cared for his unborn child, she felt a dangerous stirring in her heart. She'd been doing her best to ignore her feelings for him ever since she'd run away, but if he kept up his adoration of the baby, she might not have a choice in the matter.

The movements slowed, then stopped. Sadik kissed her belly, then climbed out of bed. He stood there naked, obviously unconcerned that she could look her fill. His body was darned impressive, she thought, studying the outline of muscles, his flat belly and long legs. Not that she was as old-fashioned as the prince, but she had to admit she'd hit the genetic jackpot with her baby's father.

"We will be married," Sadik announced.

Cleo stared at him. Her brain absorbed the words and promptly rejected them. Her heart jumped, and she instantly felt way too undressed to be having this conversation.

"Excuse me?"

"You are to be the mother of my child. It is right that we should be married."

A coldness settled in her bones. Cleo could barely breathe as she sat up, then slipped off the bed. She ignored Sadik as she collected her clothes.

Married? He wasn't serious. Yet she knew he was. He would marry her for the baby. Of course. Why hadn't she realized that before? For the child all things were possible. A combination of rage and hurt flooded her, making her actions jerky.

"What are you doing?" he asked as she pulled on her panties and reached for her bra.

"I would think that is obvious," she snapped. "I'm getting dressed, then I'm getting out of here. I should never have come. I'm sorry we made love."

It hurt to breathe. It hurt to keep moving. It was as if he'd attacked her with a club instead of with words. It wasn't supposed to be like this.

Cleo couldn't have said why she was so upset. She simply knew that she had to get alone and be by herself before she lost control.

"You are not going anywhere," Sadik announced, still beautiful, still naked.

She refused to look at him. "You would be wrong about that," she said as she slipped into her dress. It took a shimmy or two for her to pull up the zipper, but she managed it. She'd left her flowers at the reception. She had a very expensive necklace somewhere in Sadik's rooms, but she would worry about that another time. After slipping into her shoes, she headed for the door.

He stalked over and grabbed her arm. "You are not going anywhere," he repeated, obviously annoyed by her reaction. "I have said we are to be married. It is a great honor. You will be my wife, a princess of Bahania. How dare you not be pleased.''

She jerked free and glared at him. "To be honest, Your Highness, I'd rather eat glass.''

She opened the door and stepped into the hallway. Sadik spluttered, but he wasn't dressed to give chase.

At first Cleo walked, but after a couple of minutes, she slipped off her shoes and ran down the long corridors. She made her way back to her suite and let herself in.

When the door was safely closed and she found herself alone, her legs seemed to give way. She sank onto the floor. After dropping her shoes, she pulled her legs to her chest—as much as she could—and rested her head on her knees.

Great painful sobs welled up inside of her. She tried to hold back, then figured there wasn't much point. Who was she trying to impress?

Cleo cried as if her heart was breaking. A combination of sadness and anger fueled her emotions, and for several minutes she simply allowed her feelings to vent. When the storm had passed, she rose and went in search of a tissue.

She avoided looking at herself in the bathroom mirror. After blowing her nose, she stripped out of her fancy dress and slipped into her robe. The cotton folds were familiar and comforting. She cracked the French doors leading to the balcony, then crawled into the bed and rested her face against the cool fabric of the pillowcase.

Sadik wanted to marry her.

Just thinking the sentence made her eyes well up with tears. She started to get angry again.

"What's going on?" she asked aloud.

There wasn't an answer. Only the faint sound of music from the reception still going strong. Cleo curled up, feeling alone, lost and confused. Sadik's offering to marry her was the honorable thing to do. Why did it bother her so?

She tucked her hands under the pillow as she considered her feelings. For one thing, his proposal hadn't been an offer. He'd announced they were getting married. Not that his actions were a surprise. Sadik pretty much took what he wanted and dealt with any consequences later. What was the old staying? Ask forgiveness, not permission.

Except Sadik was a prince, so forgiveness was rarely needed.

He wanted to marry her. Why was that bad? It answered her question of what was to become of her when the baby was born. In fact, now that she was able to think straight, she shouldn't have been surprised. Sadik wouldn't want his firstborn child to be illegitimate.

Cleo closed her eyes and sighed. That was it, she realized. Everything about his wanting to marry her was based on the child. It wasn't about her. If it weren't for the baby, he wouldn't have had anything to do with her—except for a possible invitation to join him in bed. Which he'd done, anyway.

It was the baby he cared about, not her. *Not her.*

Cleo rolled onto her back and stared at the ceiling. She remembered the last time she'd been here. Sadik had seduced more than her body—he'd found his way into her heart. She'd been smarter then. She'd known that there was no way she could find happiness with a handsome prince, so she'd cut her losses and headed back home.

Secretly she'd hoped he would come after her. She'd waited for the phone call that never came. Gradually she'd realized that he'd forgotten her.

But she'd been unable to forget him. Because she'd allowed herself to care and because she'd given herself to him.

A combination of parental abandonment and a big chip on her shoulder had sent Cleo into the world with something to prove. When she'd made the transition from girl to woman, her body had matured years before her emotions. All the attention she'd received in high school had been a balm to her wounded heart. She'd thought her curves were far from the ideal of thin and thinner, but the boys had adored her.

So she'd given in, because at sixteen the line between sex and love often blurred. By the time she'd turned twenty, she'd figured out that there *was* a line, but being sexually available was a hard habit to break.

When she turned twenty-one, she vowed she would never give her body unless she also handed over her heart.

Then she'd met Ian. He managed a pet supply store and they'd bonded over a particularly complex printing order. He'd invited her for coffee.

As he'd been the first man she'd met after her vow, she'd promised herself to go slow. It hadn't been difficult. Ian was sensitive and kind, about as opposite from the guys she usually dated as it was possible to be.

She shifted on the bed as the uncomfortable memories returned. She remembered laughing with Ian. Talking late into the night. She remembered sharing hopes and dreams. He'd talked about wanting to get married and have a family. For the first time ever she'd allowed herself to believe that a normal life was possible, even for someone like her.

When their relationship had moved to the next level, she'd found herself eager to make love with him. While he hadn't been all that exciting in bed, he'd been caring and attentive, if a little clumsy. She'd known she could be with him for the rest of her life.

Her bubble burst when a friend mentioned seeing Ian with another woman. At first Cleo had been too content to worry much, but eventually she'd asked him about her. Ian had told her the other woman was his fiancée.

Cleo rolled back on her side and covered her face. That moment was forever frozen in her mind. The disbelief at first. How she'd thought he was kidding, even though it was a pretty awful joke.

"I'm marrying Sandy," Ian had repeated.

"What about us?" Cleo couldn't remember being more stunned as his words sunk in. He *wasn't* kidding. This wasn't a joke.

"There's no us."

She'd been stunned by the contempt in his voice and the lack of caring in his eyes. Then he did the unthinkable. He laughed at her.

"Did you really think any of this mattered?" he asked, still chuckling. "Come on, Cleo. This was my last fling before settling down. I told you I wanted to get married and have kids.'' He looked at her as if she were the most stupid person on the planet. ''You didn't really think I was serious about you? You're the kind of woman guys sleep with, but you're sure as hell not the kind we marry.''

Even now the words burned down to her soul. Somehow he'd found out about her past, she'd thought at the time. Or maybe the truth had been there for him to see. Maybe he didn't need to know her past. Maybe just by looking at her he could tell that she was worthless.

Broken and bleeding, Cleo had gone home. She hadn't told anyone what Ian had said, but she'd been unable to forget. That night, sometime between midnight and dawn, she'd vowed to never care about a man again. No matter who he was or what he said, she wouldn't give in.

Two years after her self-imposed ban on relationships, she'd flown with her sister to Bahania, where she'd met a handsome prince. He'd charmed her and made her feel special. When he'd held her in his arms, she could tell that he thought she was amazing. It had been a temptation she'd been unable to resist.

And now that man wanted to marry her. But not for herself. Not because he loved her and couldn't imagine a world without her, but because she was pregnant with his child. Without the baby she was nothing.

Cleo forced herself to breathe slowly. She didn't want to cry again. She didn't want to feel anymore. Certainly she didn't want her feelings for Sadik to continue to grow.

Why had she given in? Why had she allowed herself to turn her back on her vow? She would pay the price for the rest of her life.

Then the truth settled on her—heavy, thick and inescapable. Her anger came from the death of her fantasy. Deep in her heart she'd wanted him to fall in love with her. Obviously, he hadn't. Instead he'd gotten on with his life. Now he was going to do the right thing and propose, but that didn't mean she mattered at all. All her hopes and dreams dried into dust. When they blew away, she would have only an ugly reality made up of two inescapable elements: a man who had married her out of duty and a heart hungry for so much more.

"Cleo?"

Cleo stirred, recognized Sadik's voice and groaned. After a sleepless night she'd finally fallen into a light doze shortly after dawn, only to awaken a half hour ago with unexpected and unwelcome morning sickness.

Having thrown up and brushed her teeth, all she wanted was a chance to sleep for the rest of the morning.

"Go away," she called, knowing he would be able to tell she'd cried long into the night. Unfortunately, despite the size of the suite, there wasn't anywhere for her to hide.

He strolled into her bedroom looking tall and fit, as if he'd rested well. He probably had, she thought bitterly. No ghosts from his past had kept him up into the wee hours. As far as he was concerned, everything was settled.

He approached the bed, then settled on the mattress next to her. He smoothed her spiky bangs off her face. "You do not look well."

"Gee, thanks."

"Rest is important for the baby."

"I know that," she said between clenched teeth. "I don't want to see you. Please leave."

He ignored her. Like that was a surprise. After taking her hand in his, he brought it to his mouth where he kissed first her knuckles, then, turning her hand, the inside of her wrist. Cleo really hated the shivers that instantly danced up her arm and then shimmied around the rest of her body.

"We will need to be married quickly," he said, as if picking up a conversation that had recently been interrupted. "The baby will come early, but that is of no consequence. The future prince will be the light of my life. My father will also be delighted. A first grandson. That is an event of great happiness here in the kingdom. It has been many years since there was a baby in the palace."

He frowned slightly. "I will have to research the correct naming of our son. There are traditions to be upheld. Also there are certain schools I wish to contact. They will hold a place for him. Do you know when the baby is due?"

She stared at him. They weren't actually having this conversation. No, this had to be some kind of strange dream or out-of-body experience.

When she didn't answer right away, Sadik just kept on talking. "When you know for sure, let me know. Not that it matters for the schools. They are always pleased to have a member of the royal family attending. The British schools are excellent, but as you are American, that might be better.''

His lips kept flapping. Cleo couldn't believe all that he was saying. He wanted to talk about schools and universities, while their child wasn't much bigger than Sadik's palm.

''You can make all the plans you want,'' she said, ''but I haven't changed my mind. I'm not marrying you.''

Sadik looked mildly annoyed. He returned his attention to her wrist where he did slightly illegal things with his tongue. She felt herself starting to melt, so she snatched her hand free of his hold and sank deeper into the bed.

''You are pregnant with my child,'' he said, as if speaking to a child. ''The firstborn grandchild of the king of Bahania cannot be born illegitimate. Nor would I allow such a thing. We will be married.'' He hesitated, then almost as an afterthought asked, ''Why do you resist marrying me?''

At last he wanted to know what *she* thought of all this. The good news was she'd cried herself out last night. This morning there just plain weren't any tears left. So she was able to listen to him go on about marrying for the sake of the baby without feeling more than a stab or two to her heart.

''You're only interested in the baby,'' she said. ''I'm willing to be cooperative, but getting married isn't an option.''

Sadik stood and glared down at her. ''I honor you by this proposal.''

"No, you honor yourself. You don't care about me at all. The baby is all that matters. Frankly, I don't see that as a recipe for happiness, so why would I want to commit to staying here with you for the rest of my life?"

Her words seemed to have genuinely shocked him. He opened his mouth and then closed it. "I am Prince Sadik of Bahania. I am proposing."

"I don't think your station in life is a big surprise to me at this point, and I got that there was a proposal on the table." She sat up and leaned against the headboard. It was time to tell him the truth...or as much as she could say without giving away too much. "I don't want to marry someone who doesn't care about me."

"We have mutual respect and passion. That is a strong beginning for a marriage." He frowned. "I will not be taking another wife. Is that your concern? Not only does Bahanian law forbid it, but I find you difficult enough."

She supposed that was something.

They were at an impasse. Bottom line—he'd given his heart to Kamra and it was no longer available. Even if it was, she was hardly going to be his first choice for happily ever after.

"Mutual respect and passion isn't enough, Sadik," she said gently. "You're not listening, and you're not thinking this through. I'm the wrong woman for you to marry. Can you really see me as a princess?"

"Of course."

He answered without thinking. In a way it was really sweet, but totally unrealistic.

She hadn't wanted to get into this. To be honest, she

didn't want him to know the truth about her past. But it seemed that she didn't have a choice.

She scooted over in the bed, then patted the mattress. "Have a seat."

When he settled next to her, she studied his face. His dark eyes, the sharp plane of his cheeks, the firm, stubborn jaw. What on earth had she been thinking, falling for a handsome prince? Of course, if he hadn't been handsome, the situation still would have been really complicated.

"I want to cooperate," she said slowly. "I'm resigned to staying here. I know I can't take my child and hide out from you. Not only would you eventually catch me, but it would be wrong." She drew in a deep breath. "We can come to terms about the baby, but I can't marry you."

Annoyance clouded his face. He started to rise, but she put a restraining hand on his arm. "Hear me out, Sadik."

"Women are always difficult," he muttered.

"Perhaps, but I'm being difficult for a good reason." She bit her lower lip. She tried to forget her past as much as possible. Her circumstances had nearly broken her many times, but she'd always found the courage to go on. She was going to have to do that again.

"I'm pretty sure my parents were married," she began. "I never found a marriage license, but my mother said they were, and I have my dad's name. I never knew him. He died before I was born. He overdosed on drugs."

Sadik's expression turned unreadable, but she guessed he hadn't expected to hear this kind of story.

"My mother was also an addict. She was in and out of rehab or jail for as long as I can remember. She'd usually leave me with a neighbor. Sometimes the state stuck me in foster care. Sometimes she just disappeared and I did the best I could until she showed up again."

Cleo spoke the words without considering their meaning. If she actually focused on what she was saying, the past overwhelmed her and she found herself drowning in the memories. It was far better to stay disconnected.

"There were times when we lived with her friends and times when we didn't have anywhere to go. I remember spending nights on the streets or in shelters."

"How old were you?" Sadik asked.

She didn't look at him. Instead she stared at the blanket covering her, at the weave of the cotton and the smoothness of the fibers she rubbed between her fingers.

"I don't know. Young. I remember being about four or five and hiding in a doorway. I didn't go to school much. We were always moving around the city." She smiled. "I was born in Los Angeles and lived there until I was about eleven. I'll bet you didn't know I was from the land of movie stars."

She risked glancing at him and saw she had his full attention. His dark eyes stared into hers. She looked away because she didn't want him to see too far into her soul. He would find it a disappointing place.

She cleared her throat. "Anyway, things got pretty bad. Mom was sick and then one day she died. The state bounced me around in foster care. I was labeled a problem child. I did badly in school. Then I was placed with Fiona and Zara.'' She shrugged. ''Fiona was a bit of a flake, but she had a big heart. The first thing she did was buy me all new clothes, along with a big stuffed bear. She told me I was pretty. I pretended not to care, but she was the first person in my life who ever saw me as a real person and not just an inconvenience.''

She had to pause for a second to swallow tears. ''Zara was pretty cool. She was smart and cute, but a social retard. We made a good team. She helped me with my schoolwork and I helped her to fit in. When Fiona decided to move on, she simply took me with her. I guess the state lost my paperwork or something because no one ever came looking for me.'' She shrugged. ''So that's how I came to be Zara's foster sister.''

''You survived a great deal,'' he said.

She raised her chin and glared at him. ''I didn't tell you all that to get the sympathy vote. My point is I'm hardly princess material. You have to see that.''

''What I see is someone strong enough to overcome humble beginnings. I am impressed by your ability to rise above your circumstances and become the charming, intelligent woman I see before me.''

She groaned. The man was as thick as a plank. ''Sadik, get real. I'm not smart. I barely finished high school, and that wouldn't have happened without Zara. I wanted to go to college, but I didn't think I could make it.''

''Intelligence and education often have little in common,'' he said. ''Your spirit and drive bode well for our son.''

She leaned toward him. "Are you listening to even one word I'm saying? What happens when the press finds out about my past? I promise you, they will. They'll go digging, and that's what they'll find."

"I do not care what they find. Their opinions are of no consequence to me." He took her hand in his and laced their fingers together. "You may protest all you want. You may scream and cry and tell me more stories from your past, but make no mistake, we *will* be married."

Chapter Eight

Sadik watched the battle rage in Cleo's eyes. She was both grateful and furious. Grateful that he'd accepted her past without judging her and furious that he still insisted they marry. At times women could be annoying and complex, but at other times they were very simple.

"Did you think you could frighten me off so easily?" he asked, stroking her palm. Her skin was soft and warm. Just this simple touch aroused him. He foresaw many long, glorious, *passionate* nights once they were married.

"You are *so* missing the point," she grumbled.

"Then enlighten me."

"I'm not princess material!" She practically shouted the words. "How can you want to marry me after knowing all this? It should change everything. I don't have the breeding or the training.''

''You are not a prize mare for the horse stable. A documented bloodline is not required. Your breeding is apparent in how you conduct yourself. In what you think and say.''

''Oh, sure. And I climbed right into bed with you. Hardly a recommendation to the pedigree committee.''

''I seduced you,'' he said easily.

She jerked her hand free. ''Dammit, Sadik, listen to me. You did not seduce me. There have been other men. I didn't come to you some whimpering virgin. I had a very active sexual past when I was a teenager. I confused sex with love and I was a lonely kid. I went looking for connection and meaning, and what I found was a ticket to nowhere. I figured out reality a few years ago and I vowed to keep away from a sexual relationship until I knew I really cared about the guy.''

Which meant she'd cared about him. He had suspected as much, but having confirmation pleased him. As for her past… ''I know you were not a virgin. Nor was I. I have a past, as well. In an effort to show you that ours will be a successful marriage, I will not judge you in any way for your past. Now that we are together, you will be faithful only to me.''

She flopped on her side, her back to him, and covered her face with her hands. ''You are so infuriating,'' she mumbled. ''I can't stand this.''

He walked around the bed and pulled her hands from her face. ''I have told you I will not judge you for your past. I have listened to the story of your childhood and found only that which I admire. I have discovered you are carrying my child and I propose marriage. Tell me what I am doing that is so wrong.''

Her mouth worked, but she didn't speak. Sadik watched her, pleased that he had finally stunned her into silence. She could not possibly have an argument to refute his; therefore, they would marry.

In truth he was a little annoyed that she had resisted so far. Did she not realize that he could have chosen to marry anyone? Women around the world would be honored to be his chosen bride. Yet Cleo acted as if he had asked her to cut off her arm.

''Life in the palace is not a hardship,'' he reminded her. ''You will never want for anything. Your sister will be close, and I will allow you to visit her as much as you would like.''

He hesitated, not sure he wanted to give away so much. He reasoned that once the baby arrived, however, Cleo would not be eager to make the journey to the City of Thieves.

''You may shop in the finest stores in the world. You will have dazzling jewels to wear and parties to attend.''

She raised her head and glared at him. ''Do you really think you can buy me off?''

Many women could be controlled by the privileges of wealth, but Sadik suspected Cleo was not one of them. ''You will be a princess,'' he reminded her. ''A member of the royal family of Bahania.''

Her temper eased slightly. ''I always wanted to be part of a family,'' she murmured. Then she sat up. ''But you're missing the point.''

''Which is?''

"The fantasy of being rich doesn't make up for the realty of being married to a man who doesn't care about me. You're only doing this because of the baby. That's not how I plan to start my marriage."

He genuinely did not understand. "What do you want from me?"

"I want you to say it's about more than the baby."

"Of course it is more. If I found you repugnant, I would still suggest marriage so my son would not be a bastard, but it would be with the understanding that it was a short, temporary arrangement. In a year or two, we would divorce." He straightened. Now it was his turn to be annoyed. "I am not suggesting that. I am offering a genuine marriage, with all the commitment that entails."

Her blue eyes flashed with scorn. "I don't believe you for a second."

The challenge delighted him. He moved close and bent low to kiss her mouth. "I can prove it," he murmured, instantly aroused and ready to make love with her. It was always like this when they were together, he thought contentedly.

Instead of responding passionately, she pushed hard on his shoulder, momentarily forcing him to step back. Cleo then slipped off the bed and headed for the bathroom.

"I won't marry someone who doesn't love me," she announced loudly, stepped into the bathroom and slammed the door shut behind her. Sadik heard the distinct *click* of a lock being turned.

He glanced from the door to the bed and back. What

had gone wrong? Why did she speak of love? Then he shook his head and walked out of her bedroom.

"Women," he growled. "They are not worth the trouble."

Cleo spent the morning pacing the length of the living room in her suite. She figured if nothing else, she was at least getting a workout. That had to be good for the baby, even if the worrying wasn't.

Every time she thought about what she'd told Sadik, she wanted to die from embarrassment. Just thinking about her final words was enough to make her cheeks heat and her palms grow sweaty. Worse, she hadn't known what was in her heart until she'd spoken the words.

She was an idiot. Unfortunately, she was also doomed to a life of unhappiness.

I won't marry someone who doesn't love me.

The statement echoed in her head, repeating itself over and over again. She hadn't meant to say that, hadn't meant to even think it. She also hadn't meant it to be true.

There was only one reason that Sadik's affections mattered so much. This wasn't about pride or station or being happy or even what was right. It was about her heart.

She loved him.

Cleo didn't know when or where she'd been foolish enough to fall in love with an emotionally inaccessible royal prince who, by the way, was still in love with his dead fiancée.

What on earth had she been thinking? She stopped

in midpace and drew in a deep breath. She hadn't been thinking. She'd been feeling and dreaming and hoping, and she'd been darned stupid.

Now she was trapped by circumstances she couldn't control. She would fight the wedding for as long as possible, but what if she didn't win? What if she really had to marry Sadik? She would spend her life in love with someone who wouldn't love her back. It was her worst nightmare come to life.

She crossed to the sofa and sat. The pain she'd felt when Ian had told her that she was the kind of woman men had affairs with but didn't marry was a pinprick when compared with the ache of living with and loving Sadik, all the while knowing he was in love with the one woman he could never have.

She wrapped her arms across her chest, as if to hold in the bleeding. The only bright spot on her otherwise bleak horizon was that Sadik was too self-centered to guess what her declaration had meant. He would probably think that she was demanding love in the way of selfish women. He wouldn't think that she was actually already in love with him herself.

Small comfort, she thought glumly, but she would cling to it, as it was all she had.

There was a knock on the door of her suite. Cleo straightened, then braced herself for another altercation.

"Come in," she called.

The door opened, but it wasn't her prospective bridegroom who entered. Instead a very confused Sabrina walked inside.

The king's youngest daughter looked elegant as always in a black pantsuit with a teal shell. She wore her hair piled up on her head.

Cleo rose. "I thought you and Kardal were heading home today," she said.

Like many of those attending the wedding, Sabrina and Kardal had spent the night in the palace.

Sabrina nodded slowly. "Kardal already left for the city, but I stayed behind. Sadik came to see me while I was packing." Her gaze dropped to Cleo's midsection.

Cleo wanted to cover herself. In the past week she seemed to have doubled in size, as if the baby developing inside of her had had a growth spurt. The dress she wore had been loose at one time, but now it stretched tight over her belly, making her condition more than obvious. She would never have worn the garment out of the suite, but as she hadn't been expecting visitors, she'd pulled it on that morning after her shower.

She put one hand on her belly. "I guess this sort of says it all."

Sabrina nodded. "When Sadik told me about the wedding, I'll admit I was surprised. I knew there was something between the two of you but I didn't know it was serious. Then when he mentioned the baby, I realized—"

"He what?" Cleo knew she was interrupting a princess and that it was probably considered bad form, but she couldn't stop herself. "He said we were getting married?"

"That's why I'm here," Sabrina admitted. "To help with the wedding. He said we would have to move quickly.'' She eyed Cleo's stomach. "How far along are you?''

"I'm a week into my fifth month.'' She circled the sofa and walked over to Sabrina. "Look, I appreciate you coming here, but I have to tell you, there's not going to be a wedding. Not now, not ever. So if you want to head back home with your husband, I suggest you do so.''

Sabrina shook her head. "This is worse than I thought.'' She took Cleo's arm and led her back to the sofa. "Let's sit down and we'll start from the beginning. Obviously, there's more going on than Sadik let on.''

"I'll just bet,'' Cleo muttered.

As she plopped onto the seat cushion, she realized that Sabrina's surprise meant the king hadn't told everyone about her pregnancy. Only a select few. Zara and…

She swallowed. Sadik, she thought, suddenly breathless. And if the king told Sadik, he had to have a reason. Which meant he already knew who was the father of her baby. Which meant the situation had just gotten a little more complicated.

"Okay,'' Sabrina said, angling toward her. "Obviously, you and Sadik got involved when you were here five months ago. If you're pregnant, there must have been a spark.''

"There was plenty of that,'' Cleo agreed. "There still is, but that's not the point.'' She opened her arms, her palms up. "Look at me. I'm not even close to princess material. I don't know anything about your country or your customs. I'm a protocol disaster. Zara might have been ignorant about a lot of things, but she turned out to be an honest-to-goodness princess. I'm some kid from the streets who barely scraped through high school. Trust me, this is not someone you want in the palace.''

Sabrina smiled. ''You're being a little hard on yourself. You're a beautiful, articulate woman. Zara and I have spent dozens of hours hating you for your curves. You're also a good friend and from what I hear a great sister. Why wouldn't you fit in here?''

Cleo tried a different approach. ''Sadik and I would be miserable together. We have nothing in common.''

''You have enough to make a baby.''

''Passion fades.''

''What about love? That endures.''

''He doesn't love me,'' Cleo said flatly.

She was grateful when Sabrina didn't ask the obvious question as in, Did she love Sadik? Instead she said, ''I'm guessing my brother doesn't know what he feels right now. Things change over time.''

Cleo wanted to believe that was true. Would Sadik eventually come to care about her? Was that hope enough to build a marriage upon?

''I just don't think I can marry him.''

Sabrina's expression turned serious. ''Cleo, my brother asked me to help you plan your wedding. I'm happy to do that. In fact, I'll do anything I can to help. But if you don't want to marry him, you don't have many options. We're talking about the child of the royal family.''

''I'm familiar with Bahanian law,'' Cleo said stiffly. ''I also know that exceptions can be made.''

Sabrina's good humor returned. "I know. I'm walking, breathing proof of that. But while my father was willing to allow me to be raised outside of the country, there's no guarantee that he'll let you take his first grandchild away. I wouldn't count on making that your backup plan."

"I know." Everywhere she turned Cleo felt trapped. "I just can't deal with this now. In the end I may have to marry Sadik against my will, but I'm going to fight it as long as I can."

Sabrina gave her a brief hug, then rose. "Fair enough. I'm going to head back home. When you're ready to plan the wedding, give me a call. I'll drop everything and come here."

Sabrina headed for the door. When she reached it, she glanced over her shoulder. "I know I'm not Zara, but if you need someone to talk to, I'm happy to be available."

"I appreciate that. Thank you."

Sabrina left. Cleo flopped back on the sofa. She supposed one of the perks of marrying Sadik was that both Zara and Sabrina would become legal relatives. They would be her sisters-in-law.

Like that was enough to get her to change her mind.

Shortly after three that afternoon, Cleo received a phone call telling her she had a visitor from the American Embassy waiting for her.

She didn't understand what that could mean, but instead of arguing with the secretary on the phone, she quickly changed and made her way to the front of the palace. There she was shown into a spacious anteroom that held several leather sofas positioned around a low coffee table.

A tall man was waiting. He wore a navy suit and carried an expensive-looking briefcase. When he heard her enter, he turned and smiled, holding out his hand.

"Ms. Wilson, I'm Franklin Kudrow, attaché to the American Embassy."

Cleo was tired from her night of tears. She offered her most cheerful smile, then spoke the truth. "While that's a really impressive title, I have no idea who you are or why you're here."

"Yes. Of course." He motioned to the sofas.

Cleo settled down into one, while Mr. Kudrow settled opposite her. Manners, she thought suddenly.

"Ah, would you like something to drink?" she asked the fifty-something career diplomat.

"No, thank you." He smiled and set his briefcase on the floor. "Ms. Wilson—"

"Cleo," she said. "Just call me Cleo."

He nodded. "Cleo, we've been notified by the palace of your upcoming marriage to Prince Sadik."

Old Frank kept talking, but Cleo was having trouble listening. *Marriage to Sadik?* Word sure had traveled fast.

Anger filled her. If Sadik couldn't get her to agree the old-fashioned way, he was going to do his darnedest to manipulate her from all sides. He was a master at maneuvering his way through tricky financial markets. No doubt he thought she would be just as easy to get around.

She noticed that Mr. Kudrow was careful not to look at her stomach. His discretion was probably one of the

An Important Message from the Editors

Dear Reader,

Because you've chosen to read one of our fine romance novels, we'd like to say "thank you!" And, as a special way to thank you, we've selected two more of the books you love so well, plus an exciting Mystery Gift, to send you absolutely FREE!

Please enjoy them with our compliments...

Pam Powers

P.S. And because we value our customers, we've attached something extra inside...

Peel off seal and Place inside...

EDITOR'S FREE GIFT SEAL THANK YOU

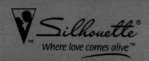

The Editor's " Thank You" Free Gifts Include:

- Two BRAND-NEW romance novels!
- An exciting mystery gift!

PLACE
FREE GIFT
SEAL
HERE

YES! I have placed my Editor's "Thank You" seal in the space provided above. Please send me 2 free books and a fabulous mystery gift. I understand I am under no obligation to purchase any books, as explained on the back and on the opposite page.

335 SDL DNTT

235 SDL DNTN

(S-SE-06/02)

FIRST NAME	LAST NAME

ADDRESS

APT.#	CITY

STATE/PROV.	ZIP/POSTAL CODE

Thank You!

DETACH AND MAIL CARD TODAY!

The Silhouette Reader Service™ — Here's how it works:

Accepting your 2 free books and gift places you under no obligation to buy anything. You may keep the books and gift and return the shipping statement marked "cancel." If you do not cancel, about a month later we'll send you 6 additional novels and bill you just $3.80 each in the U.S., or $4.21 each in Canada, plus 25¢ shipping & handling per book and applicable taxes if any.* That's the complete price and — compared to cover prices of $4.50 each in the U.S. and $5.25 each in Canada — it's quite a bargain! You may cancel at any time, but if you choose to continue, every month we'll send you 6 more books, which you may either purchase at the discount price or return to us and cancel your subscription.

*Terms and prices subject to change without notice. Sales tax applicable in N.Y. Canadian residents will be charged applicable provincial taxes and GST.

If offer card is missing write to: The Silhouette Reader Service, 3010 Walden Ave., P.O. Box 1867, Buffalo, NY 14240-1867

BUSINESS REPLY MAIL
FIRST-CLASS MAIL   PERMIT NO. 717-003   BUFFALO, NY

POSTAGE WILL BE PAID BY ADDRESSEE

SILHOUETTE READER SERVICE
3010 WALDEN AVE
PO BOX 1867
BUFFALO NY 14240-9952

NO POSTAGE
NECESSARY
IF MAILED
IN THE
UNITED STATES

reasons he'd risen in the State Department. Then she focused back in on what he was saying.

"Who told you I was marrying Sadik?"

Mr. Kudrow looked startled by the interruption. He bent down and retrieved his briefcase, which he set on the coffee table. After opening it, he drew out a piece of paper.

"We received a press release."

She took the paper and scanned it. Sure enough, there on official royal Bahania letterhead was the announcement of Prince Sadik's marriage to Cleo Wilson, an American citizen.

She couldn't believe it. That he would go behind her back like this. Did he really think he could force her hand by going public?

"We're all very excited," Mr. Kudrow was saying. "When we found out that Zara Paxton was actually a member of the royal family, we saw an opportunity to continue to cement our relations with King Hassan. Now with you marrying into the royal family, we will have even better relations. I'm sure you're aware of the proposed air force. The official position of the United States is that of neutrality, but I can tell you that privately the government is very supportive. Our government has long been an ally of the Bahanian government."

He paused expectantly. Cleo had no clue as to what he expected her to say. She went with a noncommittal grunt.

"Of course, there is hope in the private sector that many of the military planes required will be purchased from American companies. There are already several dozen orders in. Perhaps, if you have the chance to mention the quality of the American fighter jets…''

His voice trailed off, but Cleo got the message. ''Maybe I could ask for an F-14 for a wedding present,'' she said sweetly, when all she wanted to do was throw something. Instead she clutched the press release tightly in her hand.

''May I keep this?'' she asked.

''Of course.''

She rose, forcing the diplomat to do the same. ''I understand what you're trying to say,'' she told the man. ''I appreciate that my impending marriage could greatly benefit a lot of people. But here's a news flash, Mr. Kudrow. I haven't accepted the prince's proposal. So I wouldn't start counting your jet orders just yet. Thank you so much for visiting.''

She nodded once, then turned and left the room. She was furious. No. Furious didn't begin to describe how she felt. She was enraged. Now she *really* wanted to take the king up on his offer of a flogging, but only if she would be the one wielding the whip. If she had a car handy, she would back it over Sadik. How dare he try to manipulate her this way?

She stalked toward the center of the palace, determined to hunt him down and tell him exactly what she thought of him. Unfortunately, he was in the business section of the palace and she'd never been there.

After a couple of false starts, she found herself amidst dozens of fax machines and computers. Figuring she had to be close, she found a male secretary and asked directions to Prince Sadik's office.

Less than two minutes later she barged in on him.

He sat at his desk, staring at his computer screen. When she stalked into his office, he didn't even have the grace to look surprised. Instead he rose, smiled pleasantly and spoke.

"Cleo! How nice of you to come see me."

She narrowed her gaze as she slapped the press release on his desk. "Don't you dare try polite conversation on me. You might be some high-and-mighty finance person for the royal family, but to me you're nothing but a lying weasel dog. What is the meaning of this?"

He ignored her insult and glanced at the paper. "I would think it was obvious."

"That's right. It is. If you can't get me to agree another way, you're going to bully me into marrying you. Well, it's not going to work. I won't be manipulated. I don't care that you're Prince Sadik. I'm a person and I have rights."

He motioned for her to take a chair. She didn't want to give him the satisfaction of agreeing, but she was so mad, she was shaking. Her legs felt as if they were about to give way, and falling wouldn't make her look very determined.

She sank into the leather chair. He followed suit, then placed his hands on his desk. "You're making too much of this," he said calmly. "Why deny the inevitable? We *will* be married."

"No, we won't. I don't want to marry you. I have no interest in—"

He cut her off with a shake of his head. "You may protest all you like, but you cannot escape the truth. You carry my child, Cleo. You carry a royal prince.

Your choices are to marry me or to have the baby and then leave Bahania.''

He spoke the words in a flat tone of voice. She heard them, absorbed them, then clutched the arms of her chair as the room began to spin. There it was. The bald truth at last.

Marry Sadik or lose her baby.

''You couldn't do that,'' she said between suddenly dry lips. ''You're not a monster. Why would you take my child away from me?''

He rose and came around the desk. He took the chair next to hers and pulled it close. ''I have no wish for you to be apart from our child. I have told you, I want us to be married and live together as a family. You are the one who insists on making things difficult.''

Her chest tightened, and it became impossible to breathe. This couldn't be happening.

She had to reason with him, make him see that what he was doing was crazy. Panic welled up inside of her, but she ignored it. Now was the time to keep a clear head.

''Why do you want to marry someone who is so determined *not* to be with you?'' she asked, staring at him intently. ''There are many other women who would be thrilled to be your wife. Can't you marry one of them instead?''

''You are the mother of my son.''

''But don't you want a wife who cares about you?''

He smiled. As she watched, his mouth turned up and he gazed at her as one would gaze at a precious child. She wanted to slap him.

''You care about me.'' He took her hands in his. Her

fingers felt like ice, while his were warm. The contrast burned her skin. "You would not have come to my bed if you didn't care."

He shook his head when she started to interrupt. "I understand what you said about your past. That time is finished. You are a different person now."

She knew she was, but she hated that he knew it, too. It fed his argument rather than her own.

"We like each other," he continued. "We have passion, we'll have the baby. In time there will be more children. I believe we will have a long and happy marriage."

Her heart died a little as he spoke. "You want convenience," she said before she could stop herself. "You want to be sensible and do the right thing. But you don't want to love me."

The words hovered in the room like a mist. Sadik stiffened, then released her hands and leaned back in the chair.

"Is love so very necessary?"

He asked the question casually, but she would swear she heard pain in his voice. Her chest tightened.

"Yes. I don't want an empty union."

"Is it not enough I offer you the world?"

She didn't want the world; she wanted him. Only him. She loved him, and it was clear he didn't love her back.

"Sadik—"

He rose to his feet and walked to the window. Once there, he stood with his back to her. "I will tell you of love. I will tell you that it adds nothing and causes only pain."

He was wrong, but she found it impossible to speak. Silence filled the room. Then he took a deep breath.

"My engagement to Kamra was arranged. I had met her a few times and had no objection to the union. She was attractive and from a good family. Her quiet nature soothed me. She had been raised to be the wife of an important man, and as such had not been out in the world very much."

His words were daggers to her heart. Cleo doubted that she and the precious Kamra could be more opposite. But she didn't stop him from speaking. She knew she had to hear everything.

"As she was very young and not used to the ways of the world, our engagement was to last a year. Over the months we spent much time together. I grew to admire her, then care about her. Eventually I fell in love with her."

Cleo wanted to cover her ears and scream so she couldn't hear him. Her eyes burned, but she refused to give in to tears.

He shoved his hands into the front pockets of his trousers. "We quarreled. I do not recall the reason. It was barely three weeks before the wedding and she was leaving for Paris with her mother. They were to do some last-minute shopping. Kamra left in tears."

He paused for several seconds, then continued. "After a time I decided to go after her. I called ahead to delay the plane, then drove toward the airport. On the way I saw a car accident. The ambulance was already there. I slowed to give way, then recognized the car.

Her mother escaped with only minor injuries, but Kamra was dead.''

He turned to look at Cleo. His eyes were bleak, his mouth a straight line. ''My heart died at that moment, with Kamra. I will never love again.''

Chapter Nine

Cleo didn't remember leaving Sadik's office. She didn't remember anything until she found herself wandering the halls of the palace. Her whole body hurt, and she had the feeling that she would never feel whole again.

She stopped and rested on a small bench in an alcove. Misery filled her, but it was not the kind to be eased by tears. She hurt too much for that.

She forced herself to keep breathing and stay calm. For the sake of the baby, she told herself, touching her stomach. But nothing about her situation felt possible. How could her life have come to this? One of the palace cats strolled by. She tried to distract herself by petting it, but despite the feel of soft fur against her fingers, her tension didn't ease.

Was she really to be forced into a marriage with a man who didn't love her? Who *wouldn't* love her because he'd already given his love away to a woman who had died? It didn't seem possible. She wasn't completely helpless. She had a brain and she wasn't afraid of hard work. She could simply slip out of the palace and...

And what? Cleo turned the question over in her mind. Her savings back home were fairly meager and not enough to keep her going while she was on the run. She was already in her fifth month of pregnancy. How long would she be able to work? And even if she could find a well-paying job where no one asked any questions, what about when the baby came? Did she want to spend her life hiding out?

Cleo wasn't sure of many things, but she was convinced that Sadik would come looking for the baby, if not for her. Should he find her, he would take the child from her. She doubted any American court would side with her once they found out that not only had Sadik offered to marry her, he'd promised to treat her like...well...like a princess.

No one would understand, she thought sadly. No one would get that it wasn't about wealth and privilege, it was about finding love. She couldn't marry a man who didn't love her.

Cleo rubbed her temples, as if she could ease her pain. The worst part of it was that while Sadik was obviously capable of love, he wasn't willing to love *her*. She wasn't enough to bring him out of mourning for Kamra.

All her life she'd never been enough. Her mother

hadn't cared enough to stick around: drugs had been far more important than her child. Fiona had taken Cleo in but hadn't bothered to adopt her. Ian had been willing to sleep with her but had never considered her more than a plaything. Sadik was at least willing to sleep with her and marry her. She supposed that was a step up. She should be grateful. She should think it was enough.

It wasn't.

Cleo rose suddenly. There was only one last place of refuge for her dilemma. Only one person who could help her.

She hurried back to the business wing of the palace and found her way to the foyer of the king's chambers. She announced herself to one of the three male secretaries sitting behind large desks and tried not to be intimidated by the armed guards standing at attention. Her name was given to another secretary in the inner sanctum. She was asked to wait.

King Hassan kept her cooling her heels less than ten minutes. She'd barely managed to control her hyperventilating when one of the huge double doors opened and she was escorted into the king's private suite of offices.

As she followed a man in a perfectly tailored suit, Cleo tried to get a grasp of her situation. Here she was, in Bahania, about to have a one-on-one with a king. Her mind reeled at the thought. What twisted set of circumstances had brought her to this place? She was Cleo Wilson, night manager of a copy shop in Spokane. She did *not* hang out with kings.

Hassan was on the phone when she was shown into

his office. He motioned for her to take a seat on the sofa in the corner. Cleo stumbled toward the leather and sank down. The office was massive, at least a hundred feet square. Huge windows looked out over a sculptured garden. There were paintings and tapestries on the walls.

The king hung up the phone, rose and joined her on the sofa.

"I was speaking with my son, Reyhan. He is back from the oil conference." Hassan smiled. "My sons make my life easy. They take over many of my responsibilities, leaving me free to speak with beautiful women." He leaned forward and took her hand in his. "How are you feeling, Cleo?"

"I'm, ah, fine." She cleared her throat. "From what I can tell, the baby is healthy. However, I'm getting close to the time for my next checkup. I guess I'm going to have to find a doctor here and send for my records."

The king nodded. "We have many wonderful medical facilities in Bahania. Of most interest to you, I suspect, is the International Hospital. It is only a few miles from the palace and is considered a world-class facility. I believe there are several women doctors on staff."

Cleo hadn't had a chance to think about the logistics of giving birth in Bahania, but should she be trapped here, the thought of a woman doctor eased her mind.

"That would be great," she admitted, not telling him that her greatest hope was that it wouldn't be an issue. Given a little luck, she would be back home in the next couple of days and could see her regular doctor.

"Your Highness," she began, "there's something I need to talk to you about."

He released her hands, but continued to lean forward, as if showing he was attentive. "Of course, my child." He smiled kindly. "Before you begin, I must tell you how pleased I am by how things have worked out. Perhaps it would have been better if my son had not given in to temptation." He glanced at her stomach, then returned his gaze to her face. "However, I cannot complain about the outcome. Sadik is the first of my sons to provide me with a grandchild. To you that may not seem like such a great accomplishment, but I can tell you that as one grows older one becomes concerned about the future generations. I want to know that the royal succession will continue."

She didn't like the sound of that. While she appreciated the king's concern, she wished he were just a little less interested in her baby.

"Yes, well, I understand that you want your sons to have children. Or even Sabrina or Zara."

Hassan shrugged. "Sabrina's firstborn son will be heir to the City of Thieves. As for Zara, Rafe is not a prince. So you see, Sadik is the first to give me my heart's desire."

Cleo pressed her hands together. "When I told you I was pregnant, how did you know that Sadik was the father? I found out you only told Zara and Sadik about the baby."

Hassan smiled. "I told your sister because I knew she would be gone for a time on her honeymoon. I felt that things would occur while she was gone and that she needed some warning. Also, you needed a friend, and who better than a sister?''

She couldn't complain about his logic. ''Good point.''

''As for Sadik, I had seen the two of you together when you had been here before. There was something in the way you looked at each other that made me wonder what was occurring between you.''

Cleo sighed. She'd been falling in love, while Sadik had been enjoying her favors in bed. Not exactly a recipe for happiness.

''But I might have been a month or so along,'' she reminded him. ''The baby *could* have belonged to someone else.''

Hassan shrugged. ''I had no way of knowing that. I told my son so that if the child *was* his, he could make provisions. If the child wasn't his, then he needed to know not to get involved with another man's woman.''

She wanted to ask what made him think that Sadik would want to get involved with her again, but what was the point? She was stalling because she was afraid to tell him why she'd come to see him.

She cleared her throat. ''Your Highness, I mean no disrespect. I understand the honor bestowed on me by your son. He is Prince Sadik of Bahania and I'm...well, I'm no one.''

Hassan frowned. ''Cleo. You are the daughter of my heart. You have great value.''

Apparently not enough value. After all, Sadik wasn't willing to love her.

''I can't marry him.''

She spoke forcefully, and when she finished, the words hung in the air. Hassan studied her face.

"Are you married to someone else?"

"What? Of course not. If I was married, I never would have slept with him in the first place." She blushed slightly, thinking that one probably didn't discuss sex with the king.

"Then I do not understand."

Typical. Bahanian men seemed really slow on the uptake where her preferences were concerned.

"Sadik doesn't love me. He's made it very clear that he gave his heart to his late fiancée, and he has no intention of falling in love again." She paused to gather her thoughts. "I know that sounds like a silly thing to you, but it's very important to me. I don't want to be with someone who doesn't care about me. It's a horrible way to live a life."

Hassan nodded. "My son can be stubborn and difficult." He smiled slightly. "I believe he takes after me. But he will come around in time."

"What if he doesn't? You're condemning me to marriage with a man who won't care about me."

"He cares. Sadik was most distraught when you left."

She wanted to believe the king, but she had a feeling he was only saying things she wanted to hear. She decided to try a different argument.

"There are things in my past that make me unsuitable for all this. I'm afraid I would be an embarrassment to the royal family."

"We will stand together against any adversity," Hassan promised. "We will protect you."

"I don't want protection," she announced. "I want to go home. Your Highness, please. Don't make me do this. I won't keep Sadik from seeing his child, but I don't want to marry him, and I don't want to stay here."

Hassan straightened. His dark eyes seemed just a little less kind. Her stomach sank slightly. She wasn't completely stupid—she already knew that she'd lost.

"Cleo, Bahanian law is very clear. A royal child cannot leave the country. He must be raised here."

"But you could give special permission. You let Sabrina be raised elsewhere."

The king winced. "I did that in a moment of great anger, and I have had cause to regret it these many years. Those were different times and different circumstances. I will not deprive Sadik of his child. Selfishly, I will not deprive myself, either. Besides, I would miss you if you were to leave."

Cleo wasn't surprised. In her heart she'd always known that it would come to this. She tried to find comfort in the fact that she'd done her best. But as she thanked the king and started to leave his office, she couldn't help shuddering. Maybe it was crazy, but she would swear that she could hear a cage door slamming shut. Her days of freedom were over.

Sadik took several phone calls after Cleo left, but when he was finished he found himself unable to concentrate on his market predictions. Once again she'd invaded his brain and made him think of things he did not want to consider.

How could she speak of love? That was not to be

part of their agreement. They would have passion and respect. They would raise their children together, although he knew that Cleo would resist his ideas, and instead expect him to bend to her will. They would argue, she would defy him, and in the night they would make up with sweet lovemaking.

Why did she insist on bringing love into the mix? He had loved once. Kamra had been all he'd ever wanted in a wife—gentle, silent, deferential. She had honored his wishes, understood the ways of Bahania and had never questioned him. Her quiet beauty had soothed him. With her he had been able to concentrate when required. He could easily put her out of his mind. And when she was gone, he had been stunned to find himself feeling empty and alone.

Yes, he had loved once and it had taught him to never be that vulnerable again. If he had felt such grief over losing Kamra, what would happen if Cleo ever—

He pushed the thought away, refusing to consider it. Better to work, he told himself, returning his attention to his computer screen.

But before he could lose himself in his work, his secretary buzzed him to say that his father was here. Hassan walked into his office and took the chair opposite his.

Sadik nodded, then waited for the king to speak. His father obviously had something on his mind.

He was not kept waiting long.

"Cleo has been to see me," Hassan said without preamble. "She begged me to let her return home."

Something cold stirred in Sadik's belly. "Her home

is here. We are to be married and our son will be raised as my heir.''

His father waved a hand. ''I do not need convincing. I have no desire to see my grandchild living half a world away. He will be the first of a new generation. He must know our ways.''

''I'm glad we are in agreement,'' Sadik said, relaxing a little. If the king had refused Cleo's request, then she had no choice. She would marry him and they could get on with their lives. He found himself anticipating living with her. Sharing quarters with the sharp-tongued beauty would never be dull.

''There is more,'' his father said. ''While I have not allowed her to leave, I have been left to wonder why she is so convinced she will be unhappy here.'' His gaze narrowed. ''I know your relationship began out of passion, Sadik, but there is more to that woman than what you will find in bed. Cleo is very special and I expect you to treat her as such.''

''I agree,'' Sadik said easily. ''I have told Cleo that our union will be very successful. I will be loyal to her and our children. She will want for nothing. While she had indicated there are some difficulties with her past, I am not concerned. Once she is my wife, no one can hurt her.''

''All that is well and good,'' Hassan said, ''but is it enough?''

''What more could there be?''

''You have to make her happy.''

Sadik stared at his father. ''She will be my wife and the mother of my children. That is happiness enough.''

Hassan didn't speak at first. He rose and walked to

the window overlooking the garden. "I have found joy with many women in my life," he said slowly. "But there are only two I have loved. Loving a woman makes things different, for both parties." He shrugged. "There is a lesson to be learned, Sadik, but you must discover it on your own. I will warn you not to let arrogance stand in the way of your heart's desire."

"Of course not," Sadik said, even as he dismissed his father's words. He was not being arrogant with Cleo. His plan was logical, containing much sense for both of them. They would marry and she would be happy. It was the natural order of things.

"I wish you both the best," Hassan said, turning to look at his son. "Cleo is a treasure worthy of a prince. I pray you do not lose her along the way."

The next few days passed in a blur for Cleo. Dresses were sent for her to try on. She made decisions on flowers and a menu for the reception. On the morning of the wedding, she found herself unable to eat. Instead she huddled in a corner of the sofa and wondered how she'd gotten herself in this situation.

"Knock, knock," Sabrina called as she entered the suite. "Good morning, bride girl. How are you feeling?"

"Like I want to run for the hills." Cleo looked up and smiled at Sabrina. "Do you happen to have a map with you so I'll know what direction to go?"

"Sorry. And speaking from personal experience, you don't want to head out into the desert by yourself. Bad things can happen."

Cleo thought about Sabrina's past and how in her

search for the mythical City of Thieves, she'd headed out into the desert and had come home with the love of her life.

"Oh, I don't know. Some good things happen, as well."

Sabrina chuckled, then settled on the sofa. She wore jeans and a blouse. Her feet were bare and there were large electric rollers in her hair. She touched her head.

"Ah, the glamour of being a princess. If they could see me now."

"They'd probably still be impressed."

Sabrina shook her head. "I don't think so." Her smile faded. "You don't look very happy. You don't want to marry him, do you?"

"I don't seem to have a choice," Cleo said, trying not to sound bitter. "I'm carrying Sadik's baby. A little thing like happiness doesn't seem to hold much weight when compared with several hundred years of tradition." She sighed. "Sorry. I don't want to dump my troubles on you. I actually think Sadik and I could make a success of this if he weren't so…" She paused.

"Stubborn?" Sabrina offered. "Difficult? Pigheaded?"

"Those work."

"Look, I know this isn't what you had planned. It's not anyone's first choice. The good news is Sadik is a decent guy. All my brothers are. You're going to have to figure out how to bring him to his knees. Once you do that, life will be smooth sailing."

Great. It sounded simple enough. While she was at it, maybe she could part the ocean or stop global warming. "Do you have any specific ideas on how to do that?"

Sabrina grinned. "No, sorry. I think that's information you're going to have to find out on your own."

Cleo supposed Sabrina's theory was sound—except for one small problem. Her soon-to-be sister-in-law didn't know about Sadik's claim to still love his late fiancée. Hard to bring a man to his knees when he no longer had a heart.

"I'll go and let you get dressed," Sabrina said, rising. "Just call if you need any help."

"Thanks. I will."

Cleo watched her go, then settled back into the sofa. The ceremony was at five that afternoon, with a private dinner afterward. No crew of stylists and makeup artists were needed, as her wedding wasn't going to be beamed across the world and appear on international television. Quiet was better than a circus, she told herself and almost meant it.

She closed her eyes, just for a minute, and found herself dozing off. A soft brush against her cheek awakened her. She opened her eyes and saw Sadik leaning over her.

She hated that her first instinct was to get lost in his dark gaze. Her heart pattered in her chest, her body grew weak, all because he was nearby. Loving a man was simply the pits, she thought, trying to clear her mind as she sat up.

"Is there something wrong?" she asked.

He smiled and sat close to her. "Nothing at all. I simply came by to see my bride." He kissed her mouth.

The tender caress made her want to cry. For a second she thought about pointing out how seeing the bride before the wedding was bad luck, but then she figured that since they already had so much against them, breaking that one tradition would hardly matter.

"Are you nervous?" he asked.

"No. Resigned."

"Can't you be just a little happy that you're marrying me?"

She could be a lot happy. She could do the dance of joy and exultation if he would just care about her.

When she didn't answer, he changed the subject. "What about Zara? There's still time to postpone things."

Cleo shook her head. "I know she's going to be upset that she's missed my wedding, but I also know how much she was looking forward to her honeymoon with Rafe. They're supposed to have a whole month together. When else is that going to happen in their lives? I want her to have this time, and when she gets home, she'll just have to be mad at me."

"As you wish."

Oh, sure. In *that* he was willing to be agreeable. But not in the really important stuff.

"What of your belongings?" he asked.

She pointed to the stack of boxes in the far corner of the living room. "They were delivered yesterday."

Sadik studied them. "I thought there would be more. Did you not have your own place?"

"Sure, but I didn't think we'd have much use for my furniture or dishes. I had a friend pack up my personal things. Everything else has been given away to a women's shelter.''

She'd also given up her apartment. Even though there were still several months left on the lease, she wasn't going back. Actually her landlord had been surprisingly understanding when she'd explained that she wouldn't be returning. He hadn't even charged her for the extra months. Cleo wouldn't be surprised to learn that either the king or Sadik had phoned him first to make sure things went smoothly for her, but she decided the details didn't matter.

''Will you miss your life in Spokane?'' he asked, sounding almost tentative.

''I don't yet. Ask me in a couple of months.'' When the shock of getting married had faded somewhat and she was ready to deal with the reality of life in Bahania.

''I suspect you will find much to like here,'' he said. ''And speaking of things to like...''

He reached into his coat pocket and pulled out a small, black velvet box. ''My parents did not have a love match,'' he said matter-of-factly. ''Their marriage was arranged, and I doubt that either of them was very fond of the other. However, my paternal grandparents were truly in love.''

He opened the box. Inside was a sapphire ring. ''The ring is part of a set,'' he said. ''My grandfather gave my grandmother a thirty-carat stone for their twenty-fifth anniversary. She had this ring made, along with earrings and a necklace.'' He slipped the ring on her left hand. ''I should have provided you with an engagement ring before. I'm sorry I didn't think of it until now.''

She stared at the glittering stone. The ring fitted as if it had been made for her.

Sadik sat up and reached for a wooden box on the coffee table. She hadn't even noticed it. The carved wood looked old, and when he opened it, she saw it had several small compartments, all holding black velvet boxes.

"Here are the earrings," he said, showing her double drop earrings surrounded by diamonds. As promised, there was also a stunning sapphire necklace.

Cleo fingered the jewelry. She'd worn some pretty impressive pieces during her last visit to Bahania. The borrowed finery had made her feel like a princess. But it was practically cut glass when compared with this bounty.

"Why do you want me to have this?" she asked.

He frowned. "You are to be my wife," he said, as if that explained everything. "My grandmother left me her jewels with the understanding I would pass them on." His gaze softened with an understanding that stunned her, he said, "No woman has seen these since her death, Cleo. They are only for you."

She swallowed against a sudden tightness in her throat. She wouldn't have thought he was sensitive enough to realize she was worried that Kamra, too, had adorned herself with the stunning set.

"Thank you," she whispered, overcome more by his thoughtfulness than the gift itself.

He smiled, then bent low and kissed her. His mouth was soft yet demanded that she yield to him. Had she been able to speak, Cleo would have pointed out that she had no plans to resist. Not when it felt so completely right to put her arms around him and feel his body close to hers.

When he parted his mouth, she did the same. He slipped inside her mouth, his tongue gently stroking hers. Shivers of delight rippled through her. Passion flared. They had only made love once since she arrived, and she found herself quickly warming to the idea.

But instead of taking things to the next level, Sadik broke the kiss and sighed. "I think we should wait until later," he said, sounding regretful. "Although you continue to tempt me."

Cleo accepted his decision. Her response surprised her. Had Sadik continued kissing her and maybe started touching her, she wouldn't have refused him. Even now the wanting seemed to grow inside of her. She knew it was because she loved him. But would her love save her or be her downfall?

"There is more," he said, returning his attention to the box. "As my wife, there will be many beautiful jewels for you to wear. But this one is very special. It was a gift from Queen Elizabeth, the first one, to the queen of Bahania."

As he spoke he drew a delicate and beautiful tiara out of the a velvet bag. Despite the age, the workmanship was exquisite. The white gold encircled the diamonds in a series of circles. Large, pale pearls hung down, swaying as Sadik handed it to her.

Cleo couldn't believe it. She had joked with Zara about getting a cast-off tiara or two. The elegant headpiece truly symbolized being a princess. She couldn't believe that Sadik had simply handed her one, especially not one with such an amazing history.

"Is it really that old?" she asked. "Is it safe to touch it?"

"Yes to both. Sabrina is the expert in antique jewelry. Actually the tiara disappeared for a time, taken by someone in the City of Thieves. It was only recently recovered. When I heard of it, I thought you would enjoy having it for your own. Will you wear it today?"

She nodded, because it was impossible to speak. Sadik was showing her a sensitive side she wouldn't have believed existed. Maybe this marriage did have a chance.

"There are those who say a bride is not to wear pearls on her wedding day," he said. "That her new husband will make her cry once for each pearl." He touched the lustrous orbs. "There are nine pearls in the tiara. May I only disappoint you nine times in our long life together."

Tears filled her eyes. He didn't say anything. Instead he held her close and for now, that was enough.

The wedding took place in the small chapel in the palace. There was seating for perhaps a hundred, but less than twenty sat in the ancient pews. Cleo paused at the back of the church, more nervous than she would have thought.

Sadik stood waiting at the end of the long center aisle. Candles flickered. There were no windows in the chapel, no stained-glass saints to offer benediction. No visiting dignitaries, no murmuring crowd. She stared at the man she would marry, then started forward when the organ music changed to the wedding march. She walked alone.

King Hassan would have escorted her, had she asked. He didn't come out and say so, but she knew it to be true. Cleo preferred to go to Sadik on her own. She wanted to remind herself that she was doing this of her own free will. She would not be dragged to the altar.

Her cascade of roses and starburst lilies shook slightly in her hands. Her taffeta dress rustled with each movement. She'd chosen the low-cut empire style from several gowns that had been sent over. The simple lines hid her growing belly. She wore the amazing and unexpected engagement ring Sadik had given her that morning on her right hand. They had picked out simple gold bands for wedding rings. After the ceremony she would switch the engagement ring back to her left hand. Then they would go to the reception.

Cleo didn't actually mind that the reception would be small. There would be a dinner for those who attended. No crowd of several thousand, no orchestra, no endless pile of official gifts. Her wedding couldn't be more different from Zara's, but then, neither could her marriage.

Cleo was determined to make the best of it, for herself and for the baby. A life of unhappiness would surely hurt their child.

So she walked slowly toward the front of the church, prepared to marry a man who would not love her. His tenderness today gave her a small amount of hope. If only she could figure out a way to follow Sabrina's very sensible advice. But Cleo didn't have a clue as to how to bring a man like Sadik to his senses, let alone to his knees.

Chapter Ten

Pleading exhaustion, Cleo escaped from the party shortly after dinner. She couldn't help contrasting her small, quickly arranged reception with Zara's gala affair. Of course she had no one to blame but herself for the different circumstances. Zara had been smart enough to fall in love with someone who loved her. And she'd been smart enough not to get pregnant. Cleo tried to make a joke by telling herself she would do it better next time—except she knew there wouldn't be a next time. No matter what his feelings were for her, or hers for him, she and Sadik were married, and it was going to be a union for life. She would not give up her children, and he would not want the scandal of divorce.

She paused in the hallway, unsure which way to turn. Then she remembered one of the servants telling her that her things would be moved into Sadik's suite during the ceremony. She doubted that anyone would have unpacked her boxes from Spokane and wondered what Sadik would say when he saw her rather tattered teddy bear collection. It was not likely to go with his designer-perfect interior.

Cleo made a left at the next hallway, then stopped in front of Sadik's door. Her door now, she reminded herself. Her world. Her life.

She stepped inside and closed the door behind her. She'd seen the living room of his suite at least a dozen times and yet it looked unfamiliar. She took in the dark furniture, the original paintings on the wall, the view that was similar to the one from her room. She knew that this suite was laid out differently, with three bedrooms instead of two. The master suite was larger, with two smaller bedrooms on the opposite side of the living room.

Cleo crossed in that direction. The bedroom on the left contained a home office setup. The lack of papers on the desk, along with the dust cover on the computer, told her that Sadik didn't do work in here. As his actual office was less than a five-minute walk away, it made sense that he would go there when he needed to get things done.

The second bedroom had been tucked in a corner of the palace with views of both the ocean and the gardens. A good-size alcove jutted out toward the lush foliage below. A double closet held adjustable racks.

The space was completely empty, the walls bare. Cleo wasn't sure she'd ever been in this room before, but she knew it had been emptied for the baby. She placed her hand on her stomach as she turned slowly, taking in the views and the space. It was easy to picture a crib against the far wall and a changing table between the windows. Later, when their child was older, toys could be stored in the alcove. Eventually, when there were other children—she didn't doubt that Sadik wanted many—they would have to move to one of the family suites. But for now this would be home.

Cleo crossed to the wall and touched the smooth surface. What color would be best? A pale yellow, perhaps. Or maybe she should keep them cream and put up a border print of wallpaper. Maybe something with bears to go with her collection.

She closed her eyes and imagined the sound of a baby's soft sighs. She inhaled the scent of sweet skin and powder, felt the cuddly fabrics of sleepers. Her fingers pressed in slightly on her stomach, as if she could touch her child.

"I promise I'll be here for you," she whispered, and knew that was the most important thing she could do for her child—provide him or her with two loving parents.

While she doubted Sadik's desire to care about her, she believed he would be a good and devoted father. If the price of giving her child the best start possible was her own happiness, then she would pay it.

"I wondered where you had run off to."

She heard Sadik's quiet words a heartbeat before he came up behind her and wrapped his arms around her. He rested his hands over hers on her belly.

"How are you feeling?" he asked.

"Tired," she admitted. "Confused."

"How does it feel to be Princess Cleo?"

She heard the smile in his voice as he spoke, but his question didn't feel amusing to her. Instead her eyes burned. "Nothing about this situation feels real, so I can't answer the question."

He turned her in his arms. Concern clouded his eyes. "You have the luxury of time to adjust to your new circumstances," he told her gently. "We are married now. You are my wife."

Wife. She turned the word over in her mind but couldn't make it sink in. She didn't feel like his wife or a princess or anything but a fraud. A pregnant fraud.

"As you can see, I have had the furniture removed from our son's room. Whatever you require for our child will be provided. There are decorators who are familiar with the palace. There are also several large baby stores in the city, or you may order from catalogs."

She tried to ignore the ache in her heart and focus instead on the feel of his arms around her. Being close to Sadik always gave her a sense of belonging. If she could capture that sensation now and hold on to it, maybe she wouldn't be so lost.

"How do you know about baby stores?" she asked.

"I have heard rumors. Also, I checked on the Internet. There is much information there."

"I see." She stepped away from him and studied the empty space. "I don't have any specific ideas yet. I'll think about it, maybe look at some magazines to get ideas." She glanced at him over her shoulder. "Do you wish to be consulted before I go ahead with anything?"

"We may discuss it if you would like, or you may make your own choices."

She figured he knew she was upset and was trying to be sensitive. The problem was that being sensitive didn't set well on an arrogant prince.

He moved close and took her hand in his. "While we are on the subject, I would like you to redo the rest of the suite. At your own pace, when you are ready, of course. But these rooms should be ours, not simply mine."

"Of course," she murmured. His being so darned agreeable was humorous, only she couldn't seem to make herself smile.

She thought of the boxes stacked in the living room and her few items of clothing hanging in his vast closet. How on earth was she supposed to fit in here? She was *so* the wrong person for Sadik to have married.

"What are you thinking?" he asked, his voice sounding kind.

He was being nice. Perversely, she almost wished he would go back to demanding his way. At least she understood that man.

"Just that this is all too strange," she admitted. "I don't belong here."

"You are my wife," he repeated. "You are a royal princess of Bahania. Your place is wherever you want it to be."

"As long as I don't try to leave, right?" she said bitterly.

He dropped her hand and rested his palms on her shoulders. "Cleo, we are married. I know there have been difficulties between us, but it is time to put them in the past. Let us begin again, as husband and wife.''

Anger flared inside her, fueled by a sadness so profound she thought it might break her in two. ''I appreciate what you're saying. Of course it makes perfect sense. The problem is I can't forget the truth. If I hadn't been pregnant, you would never have wanted to marry me. When I left here, you didn't give me a second thought. You never called or tried to get in touch with me. I ceased to exist for you.''

What she didn't say, but was thinking, was that while he expected her to get over the past, he had no plans to do the same. Kamra was still alive and well in his mind.

''What do you want from me?'' he asked.

I want you to love me, or I want you to let me go.

Cleo sighed. There was no point in trying to answer the question, she thought.

''It doesn't matter,'' she said, feeling tired.

''It does to me.''

''No, it doesn't.'' She shrugged free of his touch. ''I'm not a person to you. I'm a vessel to carry your child.''

''That is not true.'' He reached for her, but she backed away. Sadik sighed. ''In time you will come to see that you are an important part of my life. You will understand that I have married you with the intention of fulfilling my vows. I will respect you and desire you all the days of our lives.''

She didn't know what to say, so chose to say nothing. When he put an arm around her, she let herself be led from the room. No doubt Sadik thought the problem had been solved. All would be well now.

She walked into the living room and saw that he'd had food brought in. Several covered dishes sat on a wheeled cart.

"We had dinner at the reception," she reminded him.

"You did not eat. Come. You will find that I have ordered all your favorites."

The thought of eating made her stomach turn. "I'm not very hungry," she said. "I'm tired, Sadik. I want to go to bed."

He glanced at her. She figured he would be able to see there wasn't much of an invitation in her eyes. No doubt he'd been expecting that they would do the wild thing that night—after all, they'd only made love once since she'd come back to Bahania and this *was* their wedding night.

Sadik saw the weariness in Cleo's expression. He wasn't surprised that she was tired. There had been many changes in the past few weeks. But the hopelessness also lurking there disturbed him more. He wanted her happy for the sake of the baby. Too much sadness could not be good.

His first instinct was to order her to smile, but the ridiculousness of the instruction stopped him. He could force Cleo to do as he wished, but he knew he would have little luck making her feel as he would bid. She could be both stubborn and difficult.

Patience, he told himself. He would be patient and she would come around.

He kissed her gently on the mouth, resisting the passion that flared instantly. "Go to bed," he told her. "I will not bother you this night."

She pressed her lips together, then nodded gratefully and headed for the bedroom. As he watched her go he had the fleeting thought that she would be taking the only bed in the suite, which left him in the uncomfortable position of being a bridegroom with nowhere to sleep.

Once he was alone, he glanced around for something with which to occupy himself. The food did not interest him, nor did he want to watch a movie or read a book. He prowled restlessly through the living room, then down the hall to the two empty bedrooms. The first would be for the baby. He tried to imagine how his son would look sleeping in his crib. Sadik frowned, then tried to imagine anything about his son. He did not have contact with infants or small children, nor did he know anything about Cleo's pregnancy. He barely knew when the child was expected.

His frown deepened as he made his way to the second bedroom. The makeshift office had not been used in some time, but the computer would be adequate for his purposes and it was hooked up to the Internet.

In a matter of seconds he'd logged on to a search engine and typed in the word *pregnancy*. Far too many links came up. He chose several at random and began to read. An hour later he saw there was much to be learned. He clicked his mouse on an on-line bookstore and searched their stock. When he'd ordered a half dozen different books on pregnancy and childbirth, he returned to the various Web sites and began to read.

* * *

Cleo woke up shortly after dawn. Except for a bathroom break, she'd slept through the night, resting more deeply than she had in weeks. She might not like her current situation, but knowing her fate apparently allowed her to relax about it.

She knew it was time to make the best of a bad situation. Upsetting herself couldn't be good for the baby, and being depressed would only make her feel worse. She and Sadik were married. In her case the "for better or worse" seemed to be starting out on the "worse" end, but her complaints were her own problem. She had shelter, food and a man who desperately wanted his child. They were healthy and her future was secure. Considering all that, the dream of true love seemed a little greedy.

Sadik had been right when he'd pointed out they had passion and mutual respect. And friendship. For the most part they got along. She enjoyed his company, and she would guess he enjoyed hers. That he'd been able to let her go without once thinking about her was irrelevant.

There were worse fates than being married to a wealthy, handsome prince who didn't love her.

That decided, she got up and brushed her teeth. She was trying to decide if she wanted to eat before or after her shower, when there was a knock at the bedroom door.

Sadik let himself in before she could decide what to do. He glanced first at the empty bed, then made his way into the bedroom.

"You're already awake," he said, sounding disappointed.

Cleo was too taken aback by the tray he held in his hands to answer.

"I've brought you breakfast," he said. "Please return to bed. I will serve you."

She was so surprised she nearly stumbled. "You're serving me?"

"Yes. It will be this way every morning through your pregnancy." He set the tray on the nightstand. "Unless I have to travel for business. Then I will have one of the servants bring in your breakfast."

Cleo thought about pointing out that she was more than capable of walking to a breakfast table. Especially considering that there was one right in the suite. But his thoughtful act did a number on her hormone-sensitive emotions. She found herself fighting tears.

Rather than try conversation, and risk those tears, she simply made her way back to bed and pulled the covers up to her chin.

Sadik motioned to the tray with a flourish worthy of a magician performing a disappearing act. "Fresh fruits, all picked at dawn from the palace garden. Scones because I know you like them."

She didn't want to think about the past, but his comment made the memories impossible to resist. The first night they'd been together had stretched into the following morning. As they had both been too busy flirting the previous evening to eat, they'd been starving. Sadik had ordered up breakfast, offering Cleo her choice of several items. She'd been rapturous about the scones. In fact, he'd gotten into the habit of collecting favors from her by promising scones in return.

Her gaze slid from the plate overflowing with the

fragrant pastry to a bright purple drink in a tall glass. Her stomach turned at the sight of it.

"What's that?" she asked.

"A protein drink," he said. "I found the recipe on the Internet last night. It has many of the essential nutrients both you and the baby need. There are also several ingredients, such as ginger, to ease any lingering morning sickness."

"I felt fine until I took a look at that drink," she muttered. "Does it have to be so purple?"

He looked offended. "The color is the best part."

"Then *you* drink it."

Instead of responding, he handed her the glass. She took a sip. It actually wasn't so bad.

She was about to tell him so when he knelt by the side of the bed. Cleo nearly dropped her drink in surprise. But he wasn't done stunning her for one morning.

Sadik gently pulled down the covers until they rested on the tops of her thighs. Then he tugged up her nightgown and placed both his hands on her bare belly.

His touch was gentle, his fingers warm. Afraid she would start to like this too much and pant like a dog, she took another sip of her drink.

"I have neglected our son," he told her, glancing at her briefly before returning his attention to her stomach. "There is some disagreement as to whether he can hear and understand from the womb. As I know our child will be of a superior nature, I believe he knows when he is being addressed. As my firstborn son, there is much for him to know. I will save time by beginning his education now."

Cleo couldn't speak. She tried, but her lips wouldn't move. As she watched, Sadik leaned close to her rounded stomach.

"Welcome, my son. Your mother and I eagerly await your delivery. But as it will be several months until you are with us, I want to use this time to tell you about your heritage, both of the land and the people. You are most fortunate to be born into the royal family of Bahania. You come from a long line of good and wise rulers."

He cleared his throat. "The written history of Bahania goes back over two thousand years. While that is of some importance, the ruling family of your father first took control of the throne in the year 937. Before that, many nomadic tribes had fought for control of the land that is Bahania."

Sadik spoke easily of the history of his people and their land. Cleo sipped her drink and listened. She tried to stay detached, but it was impossible not to feel close to the man kneeling beside her bed. How was she supposed to resist him when he acted like this? She felt herself falling even more in love with him.

"Horses have always been important to the desert," he continued. "There are those who say it is the camel that tamed the wildness, but it was the horse. We will discuss that tomorrow, my son."

He kissed her belly, then pulled down her nightgown and drew up the covers.

She shook her head. "What if the baby is a girl?"

He dismissed her with a wave, then snatched one of the scones. "I am Prince Sadik of Bahania."

"I keep telling you that the title isn't really news. I'm just wondering what you'll do if we have a girl."

"We won't," he said with a confidence that made her want to both slug him and hold him so close that she could hear the beating of his heart.

She sighed. "I guess I already knew you were an arrogant prince the first time I met you."

He grinned. "You were charmed."

"Not exactly."

He kissed her mouth, then walked toward the door. "You were charmed then, and you remain charmed."

She couldn't help laughing as he left. Sadik made her crazy. He made her a lot of things. But the bottom line was—the man did charm her. Darn him.

Cleo rose and showered, then dressed for her first day as a real, live princess. With the exception of a light mist of rain falling, there seemed to be little difference between this day and the one before. Except for the ring, she thought staring at the sapphire engagement ring nestling against her gold wedding band.

There it was—proof that she and Sadik were really married. The palace was now her home.

Cleo couldn't even think that sentence without wanting to run for cover. How on earth was she supposed to live it? "Don't think about it now," she said aloud.

Instead she headed for the living room where her boxes from her former life sat waiting for her. There were also several catalogs stacked on the coffee table. She didn't remember seeing them before, so someone must have brought them in. She sat on the sofa and leafed through the various baby catalogs. There were cribs and changing tables, dressers, rocking chairs, linens, clothes and dozens of containers, toys and accessories about which she had no clue. The prices were also amazing, but then, the royal set probably didn't do much shopping at discount stores.

She found a wallpaper catalog at the bottom of the pile and flipped through the pages, wondering if her child would prefer a motif of bunnies or bears. No doubt Sadik would press for a masculine theme. She would have to stand firm that there had to be at least a small chance that the baby would be a girl.

Before she could make a wallpaper decision, the phone rang. Her heart instantly jumped in her chest, making her feel both alive and very foolish. It wasn't Sadik, she reminded herself, even as she wanted it to be him.

"Hello?"

"Princess Cleo, this is Marie. I'm one of the head housekeepers here in the palace. I'm calling to find out your preference for cleaning the suite. I can send a staff member whenever you would like. The time can be flexible or set on a regular schedule. Also, I've spoken with the main kitchen. They asked me to remind you that you are always welcome to order in a private dinner, if that would be more to your liking." Humor and friendliness filled Marie's voice. "This *is* your honeymoon, after all."

Cleo didn't know what to think. "Um, I guess dinner in the suite would be great."

"Shall I have the head chef phone, or would you prefer to contact him at your convenience?"

As she didn't have a clue as to what to order for

dinner, or even what was available, Cleo figured she'd better do some research first. "I'll, ah, call myself."

"Very well. What about the cleaning?"

"Can we pass on that today? I'll decide on the best time and get back to you in the morning."

"As you wish. Please feel free to call on me for any request. It is our pleasure to serve you, Princess Cleo."

"Thanks."

She hung up the phone, feeling as disconcerted as if she'd just had a long chat with aliens. This couldn't possibly be her world. It was insane. It was royalty. Obviously, the palace was a well-oiled machine. She would have to stay out of the ever-moving cogs so she didn't get caught in the mechanism.

Cleo tossed down the catalog and crossed to the window. The sky and water were gray in the rain. She pressed her fingers against the pristine glass and wondered what on earth she was doing here. Did she really think she could fit in as if she belonged? Her? She was absolutely the last person on the planet who should have married into a royal family.

She turned and stared at the cardboard boxes stacked in the corner. She knew what she would find when she opened them. Old tattered stuffed animals and books bought at a secondhand store. There would be clothes she would never wear again and a few pictures. Minor remnants of a very small life.

She had always thought it would be more. That somehow she could make herself matter. But that didn't seem to have happened. Now she was Sadik's wife and soon to be her child's mother. She seemed to have lost herself along the way.

A knock on the door interrupted her thoughts. This time her heartbeat remained calm. Sadik would never request permission to enter his own rooms.

She rose and opened the front door. A young woman stood holding a vase of flowers. She handed them to Cleo, gave a half curtsy, then left.

Cleo stared after her, more bemused by the curtsy than curious about the flowers. Were people really going to do that to her now? It would make life unbearable. She made a mental note to call Marie and discuss it with her, then carried the flowers into the living room and set them in the center of the table. After admiring the fragrant blossoms, she reached for the small card tucked among the leaves.

"You are welcome to join me for a late-morning tea."

The note was signed by King Hassan. Cleo glanced at the clock. It was nearly eleven. She figured she'd better hustle her butt over to the business section of the palace—it was unlikely the king of Bahania had issued the invitation on a whim.

Five minutes later the king's male secretary escorted her into Hassan's private office. A tea cart stood at the ready, and the king sat on one of the sofas. He glanced up when she entered and set his report next to him. Then he rose and walked toward her, both arms extended.

"Welcome, my daughter," he said as he embraced her and kissed her on both cheeks. "This is your first day as a member of the royal family. What do you think so far?"

''I'm still numb,'' she admitted as he motioned for her to take a seat by the cart. She assumed that was a not-so-subtle hint that she was expected to pour. She had to nudge a dozing calico out of the way before she could plop down.

''Soon you'll be bustling around the palace as if you have lived here all your life.''

She patted her round stomach. ''I'm getting too big to be bustling anytime soon. Maybe after the baby is born.'' She reached for the teapot and poured the tea into two delicate cups. The china had an oriental pattern and she didn't doubt that they were from an antique set with a long history.

''Now that I live here, I guess I'm going to have to learn something about the country,'' she said, then shook her head. ''Sorry. I didn't mean it to come out that way. I'm actually very interested in Bahania.''

''There are many wonderful books in the palace library,'' the king said helpfully as she passed him his tea. ''Or I could have one of our national historians come by and give you lessons.''

She held up both her hands. ''I think I'll pass on the private tutoring. Anything I need to learn, I can find out myself, either by reading or even visiting a museum.''

''As you wish,'' the king said. ''I would suggest you begin by touring the city. There are many beautiful and historic sites.'' He frowned. ''While a Bahanian driver's license will be obtained for you, I would ask that you not venture out on your own until you are familiar with our roads. I will have a driver assigned to you.''

Cleo wasn't sure she wanted to be escorted, but the king's comments about getting to know the city made sense. The last thing she needed was to get lost.

"I appreciate that," she told him.

He smiled. "We all wish for your happiness." Hassan hesitated. "I know that the circumstances of your marriage were not what you had hoped they would be, however I am convinced that you and Sadik can be happy together."

Cleo took a sip of tea rather than answer. She didn't think her royal father-in-law would like her response.

"You would find the transition easier if you made a life for yourself," he continued. "Sadik thinks you will be content to be a mother, but I sense you will need more. What are your interests, Cleo? Bahania has much to recommend itself."

She appreciated the show of support and interest, although she found the question a challenge. "I don't have any specific interests. I've never been a hobby and craft person and I don't play a musical instrument."

"What is the one thing you have always wanted to do and has so far eluded you?"

That was a no-brainer, she thought glumly. "I know that Zara is the smart one in the family," she said. "However, I always regretted not going to college when I had the chance. When I was in high school, I didn't study much. The classes were just something I had to endure. Now I think I could really enjoy learning about things."

He set his tea on the table in front of them and spread his arms open wide. "Why don't you try it and see what you think? I'll make an appointment with the president of the university. You can go to see the campus this afternoon.''

Cleo felt as if she'd stepped onto a rapidly moving conveyor belt. ''I don't need to meet with the university president,'' she said quickly. ''Can't I just walk around the campus, then maybe apply like a regular student?''

''Child, you are many wonderful things, but you are not a regular anything. Not anymore. You are Princess Cleo of Bahania.'' He smiled. ''Don't worry. You will grow into the title.''

Not in this lifetime, she thought, more afraid of her marriage now than she had been before walking into the room. It was one thing to worry about whether or not her husband loved her. It was another to have to deal with the reality of being an actual princess. There were responsibilities and expectations she hadn't considered.

''I'm beginning to think you are all going to regret inviting me to join the team,'' she muttered.

The king shook his head. ''I suspect that in a few months we are all going to wonder how we survived without you.''

Cleo hoped that was true…especially for Sadik.

Chapter Eleven

That evening Cleo found herself surprisingly cheerful. She actually felt anticipation at the thought of seeing Sadik, and when he let himself into the suite, she hurried to greet him.

"I had the best day," she said happily. "At first I thought it was going to be pretty miserable because it's raining and I'm not a huge fan of rain. Plus there's nothing for me to do around here, but things picked up. What about for you?"

Instead of answering, he simply stared at her. She glanced down at the front of her loose-fitting dress to see if she'd spilled something.

"What?" she asked, suddenly feeling awkward.

They were standing less than two feet apart and, as of yesterday, they were officially a married couple.

Was he expecting her to hug him or kiss him? Asking about his day was sort of wifelike, after all.

"You do not seem unhappy," he said at last.

"I'm not."

"I have not seen you any other way since I found out you were pregnant. I did not know if you had forgotten how to smile."

She couldn't tell if he was teasing or not. She sighed. "I know I've been a little crabby and difficult. I didn't mean to be. It's just…" She hesitated.

Was there any way to explain how her life had been taken away from her? As Sadik had been the one doing the taking, and as he had yet to show the tiniest bit of remorse, she didn't think he would exactly jump to see her side of things.

"I know how to smile," she said, trying for a light tone of voice. "Know any good knock-knock jokes?"

He put his arm around her, as he led her to the sofa. "Not really. Are you hungry? Maria said you had ordered dinner in tonight. Do you wish them to serve right away?"

"I can wait."

She sat next to him, angled toward him. She couldn't seem to reconcile the fact that they were really married. So this was their first postworkday husband-and-wife conversation. Should she offer to get his slippers?

"Did Marie simply inform you of my decision about dinner or did she make sure it was all right with you?" Cleo held up her hand. "I'm not trying to make trouble on our first night, I'm simply trying to figure out where things stand."

"I had reason to speak with her about something

else," he said easily. "At that time I asked her if she'd spoken with you yet, and she informed me that she had." His handsome face tightened slightly. "I have been most unfair to you, Cleo."

She felt as if she could have been knocked over with, if not a feather, then at least a very light object. A thousand snippy responses came to mind, some of them even humorous. But as Sadik was actually admitting fault in something, she thought she should try to take the moral high ground.

"Ah, in what way?" she asked casually, pretending interest in a loose thread in her skirt hem.

"We did not discuss a honeymoon."

She hadn't had time to imagine what his response might be, but she doubted she would ever have come up with that.

"You're right." A honeymoon? Did she need the stress? Not that he hadn't been sweet to think of it. "That's okay. I'm pretty pregnant, and I don't know what travel restrictions I would have."

"That is all well, but I should have considered how things would appear."

Her tiny bubble of happiness burst with an audible pop. "Great. So you don't actually *care* about going away with me. You just don't want the neighbors talking."

"That is not what I said."

"It's exactly what you said, and I think it's pretty ratty of you. This whole marriage was your idea, and if you're unhappy now, you only have yourself to blame."

He sighed the sigh of the long-suffering, then gathered her close. No matter how good it felt to be held in his arms, and how warm his body was next to hers, she refused to either relax or be impressed.

"All right," he conceded. "I phrased my thoughts badly. I don't want to start gossip that would ultimately hurt you. In addition I would enjoy going away with you. But your concern about the health of our son does you credit. Perhaps after he is born we will take a belated honeymoon."

She made a noncommittal noise in the back of her throat. She didn't want Sadik thinking he was getting off that easy.

"Speaking of doctors," she said, disentangling herself before she did something stupid like start melting, "I have an appointment with one tomorrow. And I've arranged to have all my medical records transferred."

He released her immediately and walked to the phone. "What time is your appointment?"

"Eleven."

"Good." He dialed four numbers, then waited. When the phone was answered, he identified himself, then ordered his secretary to clear his appointments from ten-thirty until one.

"You don't have to do this," Cleo said when he'd hung up. "I'm perfectly capable of going by myself."

"I do not doubt that, however I wish to speak with the doctor. I am interested in everything about your pregnancy, your health and the health of our son."

"Again I point out that we could be having a girl."

He didn't even acknowledge her statement. Instead he returned to the sofa.

"There is something else we must discuss," he said,

sitting next to her. "Initially I simply made arrangements myself. However, I reconsidered. Your temperament is not as yielding as I would desire."

"If you're trying to say I'm stubborn, that's hardly news. Otherwise, what are we talking about?"

"You are Princess Cleo, now," he said. "And my wife." Surprisingly, his expression softened. "I find everything about you beautiful and desirable."

"I know," she murmured. "I have to admit, it's your best quality."

He smiled. "It is time you dressed the part."

Cleo was neither shocked nor hurt by his words. She'd known she was going to have to change her dressing ways, and soon. Being pregnant might complicate the transformation from mere mortal to actual princess, but it didn't change it.

"So you're saying there are stores that specialize in dressing today's modern, pregnant princess?"

"Yes."

"Who would have known?"

"I will have my secretary give you the name and number if you would prefer to set up your own appointment. The boutique owner will, of course, come to the palace."

"Of course."

Cleo rose and crossed to the window. The rain had stopped for the afternoon but had returned with the sunset.

"It's really exciting," she said without turning around. "I mean the thought of getting all new clothes and being well dressed in designer stuff."

Sadik watched her closely. "You do not appear happy."

She shrugged. "I remember the first time I was here with Zara. We were given fabulous dresses to wear to a state dinner. I thought it was a great game, but Zara didn't agree with me. I guess the difference was that I was going home and she wasn't. For her the situation was very real."

"As it is real for you now?"

She nodded slowly. "I'm really grateful and everything, it's just I never planned to be a princess."

"You survived your first day. Speaking of which, you never told me what you did to occupy your time. I believe your actual words were that you had 'the best time.' Tell me what made it so."

Cleo hesitated. She wasn't sure she wanted to share her new find with Sadik. What if he didn't think she could do it? Not that his opinion mattered, she reminded herself. She might not be as prepared as she would like, but she was willing to work hard. So much of life's successes were about showing up and being willing to do the work.

"I went to the university," she said, gazing at the floor rather than at Sadik. "The king suggested a tour of the city, and part of that was through the grounds of the university."

Her enthusiasm grew as she remembered the tall, old buildings blending with modern structures. There had been treasures everywhere she looked. Small gardens tucked into courtyards, fountains, benches for reading and studying.

"I walked around and then I went inside. The library

is amazing. This very nice man took me on a tour and showed me ancient manuscripts dating back over a thousand years. Sabrina's really into that stuff, so I guess she would already know about it, but I thought it was amazing. I also—''

Sadik stood and glared at her. ''You drove through the city on your own, then went to the university and spoke with a man who is not a member of this family?''

There was no mistaking his outrage. Cleo bristled as she put her hands on her hips—what she could feel of them, what with being five months pregnant—and glared right back.

''First of all, I was not alone on my tour. I was taken around by a driver. Someone the king approves of, so don't even go there. Second, I spoke with the senior librarian at the university library. I didn't dance naked through the halls of a prison.''

''You are my wife,'' he announced, as if that explained anything.

She couldn't believe it. She'd thought that Sadik might make fun of her for thinking she could get her degree in something, but they couldn't even get that far in the conversation. He was hung up on the fact that she'd spoken with a strange man.

''You need to join the rest of the world in this century,'' she told her husband of one day. ''Here's a news flash—the time of the harem is over. You can't keep your women locked up anymore. We have gained the right to move around and—'' she placed the back of her hand against her forehead and sighed dramatically ''—we can even think for ourselves.''

He frowned. "Cleo, I do not find this humorous."

"I'll bet you don't. But here's another news flash. I don't care what you think on this subject. Because my touring the library was just the beginning of it. Hang on to your shorts, Your Highness. I might be married to you and having our baby in a few months, but I'm not willing to be tied down to this palace. I plan to go out and do something with my life."

Sadik looked as if she'd slapped him with a wet fish. "What exactly are you talking about?"

Each word was clipped shorter than a buzz cut on a new military recruit.

"I'm going to start attending classes. I want to get my college degree." She leaned toward him and set her jaw. "Don't try to stop me on this, Sadik. I'm more stubborn than you could begin to imagine."

She'd obviously caught him completely off guard. He didn't speak, didn't do anything but stare at her. Finally he shook his head and turned away.

"I forbid it."

Figures. "The least you could do is not be predictable," she said to his back. "Forbid away. I'm still going to do it."

He spun toward her, his expression outraged. "You are my wife and will be the mother of my son. That is enough for any woman."

"It's not for me. If you'd thought you were marrying some 'yes woman' who didn't have a single opinion in her empty head, you couldn't be more wrong. You may be my husband, but you're not my lord and master. I suggest you get over it."

Sadik didn't know what to say. He wasn't surprised

by Cleo's defiance. She had been difficult from the beginning. What did surprise him was her description of the empty-headed female who didn't have an opinion in her head. Unfairly, he'd instantly thought about Kamra.

Sadik stiffened. He would not have such disrespectful thoughts of Kamra. She had been perfection itself—always deferring to him, never questioning his judgment, always seeking his approval.

A small yet traitorous voice in his head whispered that, with time, Kamra's devotion might have been tiresome. At least Cleo would always be challenging.

He clenched his hands into fists. He did not want to be challenged. His late fiancée had been the most perfect of women. Losing her had been the greatest tragedy of his life. He had no right to question that.

"I will speak to the president of the university," he told her. "After that you will not be attending any classes."

"No, you won't," she said softly, despite the fire in her eyes. "Because that would mean admitting you have a problem with your wife, and we both know you don't want to do that. You're going to have to control me yourself, Sadik. Which isn't going to happen, so you're going to have to get over it."

He could feel the heat from her body. Her short blond hair was in its usual spiky disarray. While the style wasn't traditional, on Cleo it looked delightful. He stared into her dark-blue eyes, then lowered his gaze to her full mouth. Even now, when she defied him, he wanted her. He might have given his heart to Kamra, but he wanted Cleo more than he had ever wanted any woman in his life. With a certainty he did not want to acknowledge, he knew that he would always want her, until his dying breath.

He reached for her and pulled her close. Before she could protest and pull away, he pressed his mouth to hers in a demanding kiss.

Surprise was on his side. She instantly softened against him, obviously unable to resist the passion between them. Her arms came around his neck, and her body nestled against his. He felt her full breasts press against his chest and her round belly pushing against him. Her body had changed in the past few weeks. Every day he could see the differences as her pregnancy progressed. He remembered touching her stomach that morning, as he had spoken with their child.

But instead of remembering the words, or the healthy movements of their son, he was suddenly able to recall the sweet smell of her skin and how soft and smooth she'd been.

He wanted her.

Cleo found herself getting lost in the feel of Sadik's mouth against her own. The man knew how to kiss. He focused all of his amazing laserlike attention on the act of making love, and he loved slowly and with a thoroughness that left her satisfied beyond measure.

Even the simple act of kissing took on more meaning when it was with him. He explored her lips with his, then licked the seam. Before she could part to admit him—or, more embarrassing, beg him to deepen the kiss—he nibbled on her sensitive lower lip. The tiny love bites made her shiver in anticipation.

His large hands moved up and down her back, as if

rediscovering her. She felt more than a little awkward, what with being into her fifth month, but she wasn't embarrassed about him seeing her naked. Sadik had many flaws, but not worshiping her body wasn't one of them. If she had her way they would—

She pulled back and glared at him. "What exactly do you think you're doing?" she demanded.

"I was about to start kissing your neck," he said calmly, as if discussing movie plans for after dinner. "Then I thought I would lick the inside of your ear and bite the lobe. After that I wanted to start undressing you."

His words created a clear visual in her mind. One that made her swallow and fogged her head in such a way that it was difficult to remember why she was supposed to be upset.

Oh, yeah. "You are not going to distract me from my purpose," she said with less force than she would have liked. But it was impossible to generate a whole lot of anger when her body was in the process of melting at the man's touch.

"What purpose is that?" he asked.

It took her a second to remember. "You're not going to seduce me into forgetting I want to get my college degree. It's wrong of you to attempt to deprive me of an education."

He pulled her close against him. "I am not trying to distract you. I'm seducing you so we can consummate our relationship. It is long past time."

"What about my—"

He silenced her with a kiss. "Later," he murmured, his mouth settling on hers. "Later."

Cleo had a brief thought that she would protest, but then Sadik began to follow the plan he'd outlined and she figured they could fight anytime. Right now it wouldn't be so very bad to give in to his insistent attentions.

He bent down and kissed from her collarbone to just below her jaw, then licked the inside of her ear. Instantly goose bumps popped out all over. She shivered and sighed. There were, she thought as her body began to heat up and prepare for the inevitable lovemaking to follow, compensations for being married to Sadik. The physical side of their marriage would always be pleasant.

But he would never love her.

The thought appeared from nowhere. Cleo firmly shoved it away. She wouldn't think about that right now. Because if she thought about how her husband would never care about her the way he'd cared about his late fiancée, the pain would chase away all her pleasure in the moment. She felt as if she'd been alone for so long. Sadik offered warmth and a safe haven. Was it so wrong to give in to that?

His hands moving from her back around toward her breasts was answer enough. She ached for him. She felt huge and ungainly, yet she knew none of that mattered to Sadik. For reasons that had never been clear, he would think she was gorgeous in burlap.

Even as his teeth closed on her earlobe, his hands cupped her breasts. Since the pregnancy, that part of her had grown exquisitely sensitive. Her nipples puckered in anticipation of his touch.

"Tell me," he whispered, then sucked on her earlobe. "Tell me if I hurt you. I read that pregnancy can make a woman's breasts too painful to touch."

Her breasts throbbed, but not in the way he meant. If he didn't touch her more intimately, she was going to die.

"I'm fine," she managed to say. The need was so intense, she found it difficult to speak. "I stopped being that sensitive a few weeks ago."

"So it is safe for me to—"

"Yes," she said frantically, unable to keep herself from putting her hands on top of his and urging him to shift. His thumbs grazed her tight nipples, and she gasped as pleasure washed through her.

She became lost in the sensation of his fingers teasing and lightly squeezing. Fire shot through her, sailing through her midsection and settling between her legs. She was already wet. She could feel her slick readiness and the dull throbbing that signified her need for release.

Sadik wrapped his arms around her, pulling her close. He kissed her deeply, his tongue slipping into her mouth and touching hers. They stroked each other, invading, playing, dancing, needing. Cleo clung to him, wanting all that he could offer. He'd always had the ability to take her to the edge of sensual sanity. Tonight she needed to forget the real world and get lost in his passion.

She became vaguely aware that he was easing them toward the bedroom. Once they were inside, he closed the door and broke the kiss long enough to lead her to the bed. With the ease of a man confident in both his abilities and his reception, he moved behind her and unzipped her dress.

The garment slipped down her arms. She grabbed it at her waist, suddenly self-conscious about the changes in her body. She glanced at him over her shoulder.

"I'm getting pretty pregnant," she said, hating that she could feel heat flaring on her cheeks.

He grinned. "I know. I have made you so."

Then his smile faded. He circled around in front of her and took one of her hands in his. This allowed her to keep her dress over her belly *and* experience his hot kisses against her palm.

"You grow round with my seed," he murmured against her skin. "I see the changes, and each day I am more in awe of your female beauty."

He released her hand and knelt on the floor in front of her. After helping her slip out of her sandals, he gently tugged on the dress until she released it. The fabric pooled at her feet.

Cleo refused to give up her bikini briefs, but instead of wearing them up on her hips, she was forced to tuck them under her stomach. She felt stupid in her panties and bra with her big belly sticking out in front. But her husband did not seem to mind. He kissed her tight skin and licked her belly button. With gentle hands, he eased her onto the bed where he knelt between her legs. After helping her off with her bra, he slipped off her panties.

When she was naked, he began the slow, sexy dance specifically designed to drive her mad. He licked her breasts until she trembled with need. The talented tip of his tongue danced with her nipples, making her writhe on the bed. When her breathing came hot and fast, he moved lower. He stroked her stomach with his fingertips, tracing patterns that had no purpose but to make her his. Ever lower and lower, but not quite touching that one place that wept for his nearness.

He slipped away, moving off the bed where he removed his suit jacket, shoes, socks, tie and shirt. Clad only in his trousers and briefs, he returned to the bed. Annoyingly, he stayed at the end with her feet. But she knew better than to worry. He would begin his attentions soon enough. She would have her release, perhaps even several. Sadik believed in a job well-done.

He didn't disappoint her. He bent low and raised her leg slightly, so he could nibble on the inside of her ankle. From there he made his way to her knee. That innermost feminine part of her quivered in anticipation. She wanted him to touch her there, to take her to paradise and back.

"Do not question your beauty," he said, his voice low and husky. Still holding her ankle, he brought her foot against his arousal. Her arch nestled against the hard ridge of his need. When she rubbed him, he briefly closed his eyes and groaned.

"That is for later," he promised.

She smiled. "Have I confessed that I have a sexual fantasy about making you lose control?"

His eyes snapped open. A delicious expression of delight stole across his face. "Tell me the details of your fantasy."

She shrugged, pretending indifference to the question. "It's nothing really. Just that we're together, making love."

His dark eyes glittered. "Go on."

She noticed that he'd released her foot and was moving between her legs.

"We're both naked," she said, as his hand pressed against her waiting heat.

"And?"

"I start to touch you."

As she said the words, he shifted so that two fingers pressed deep inside of her. At the same time his thumb found the knot of nerves designed solely for her pleasure. He moved in a slow, steady rhythm. She swallowed.

"What was I saying?" she asked.

"You were telling me about touching."

If he was trying to provide positive reinforcement for discussing a fantasy, he was doing a darned good job, she thought, barely able to focus. He worked magic between her legs, moving in and out as he rubbed her with his thumb. The combined attentions made her tense in anticipation of her release. She could feel the pressure building and the—

"Cleo?"

"Huh? Oh, sorry." She shook her head. "I'm, ah, touching you with my hand, then with my mouth."

"I like it when you do that."

"I know." She caught her breath as he picked up speed. In and out, over and over, mimicking the act of love that would follow.

"So how do I lose control?" he asked.

"You make me stop," she said, barely able to complete the sentence. "You grab me by the hair and pull my head back. Then you plunge into me."

He didn't stop moving, but she saw the frown on his face. "Sadik, it's a fantasy."

"I would never grab you by your hair."

Despite the tension building inside of her, she smiled. "That's not the point."

"Oh, I understand the point."

He stopped touching her. She nearly cried out in protest, but before she could say a word, he reached for the fastenings on his trousers. He ripped open his belt and shoved down his clothing until his arousal sprang free. Something dark and animalistic entered his eyes.

"Your fantasy is that I can't wait," he said, pressing against her opening. "That I find you so irresistible that I forget myself and say, to hell with convention."

He slipped his fingers between them. As he began to fill her, he moved against her most sensitive place. The combination was unbearable.

"I can't wait," he told her, holding her gaze. "I *will* have you now."

She wasn't sure how much of this was about her fantasy and how much it was because having her talk about it turned him on. She found she didn't much care. She felt herself spiraling out of control. The combination of his fingers rubbing against her and his large erection filling her was more than she could stand. Pressure built until there was no way to stop the explosion.

The contractions began slowly. She arched her head back and cried out his name. The release raced through her, growing and building even as he thrust into her over and over again. The question of holding back had long been answered. It was impossible. Not while he was touching her. She felt herself opening—not just her body but her heart. When he claimed her as his, he claimed *all* of her, although she was determined never to let him know.

He shuddered and stilled. She felt him find his own way to paradise. What she didn't know was what she would do when he found his way back.

Chapter Twelve

The next morning Cleo found more than a snack waiting for her on the dining-room table in the suite. There was a Bahanian driver's license, several credit cards in her name—all platinum, of course—a checkbook with an opening balance of $250,000 and a stack of cash. She didn't bother to count it.

This was, she supposed, another perk of having recently married into the royal family. The problem was, it felt an awful lot like a bribe.

It was because of last night, she thought, still not fully recovered from the intense intimacy she'd shared with Sadik. While they had always experienced passion, something else had occurred the previous evening. Did being married really make that much difference? She didn't want to think so. Her emotional connection with her husband had already gotten her into trouble, promising her the potential of a lifetime heartache. She didn't want to make things worse by bonding even more.

At least the surprise he'd left her gave her something else to think about. She collected the driver's license, one of the credit cards and half the cash, dropped the lot into her purse and headed out the door. Ten minutes later she entered Sadik's office with the intent of putting the man firmly in his place. She might have been stupid enough to hand over her heart, but she wasn't about to let him run her life. Not when his idea of the perfect wife was someone who was silent, obedient and fertile.

"Good morning," he said, rising from his chair and coming around to greet her. He cupped her face and lightly kissed her mouth. Just the brush of his lips on hers was enough to get her all hot and bothered, although she didn't want to admit that to anyone—not even herself.

"How are you feeling?" he asked when he released her.

"Fine." The man had seen her less than two hours before, when he'd delivered breakfast and spent forty minutes talking to her stomach. It was unlikely anything had changed.

When he motioned for her to take a seat, she shook her head. "I'd rather stay standing. It's easier to work up a good head of steam when I'm on my feet."

Sadik looked genuinely confused. "Why would you want to be angry with me?"

She pulled out the wad of cash and slapped it on the desk.

"I do not understand," he said as he frowned at her. "If you require more, you may cash a check from your account. When the balance drops below one hundred thousand dollars, an additional deposit will be made. My desire is that you want for nothing."

"Which is a sentiment I applaud. But only in theory. You can't buy me, Sadik. However much money you leave on the table, I'm still going to apply to the university this morning, and you can't stop me."

Storm clouds collected in his eyes. His dark eyebrows pulled together. "You are my wife."

"Uh-huh, and if you didn't want stubborn, you shouldn't have married me." She grabbed the cash and shoved it in her purse. "I don't know how much textbooks cost. I might need this."

He stiffened. "I told you last night, I forbid you to attend the university."

"And I told you, this is about what *I* want. I'm willing to follow the rules and be a good wife. I'll have your children and support your career and attend social functions, but I won't be dictated to. Nothing about my furthering my education is going to threaten our relationship."

"What about when we have children? You will need time to be a good mother."

She rolled her eyes. "All over the world there are single moms doing a darned good job. They are employed, supporting their family, going back to school when able and having something resembling a life. I think that I can manage to raise a couple of kids while living in the palace and surrounded by hot-and-cold-running servants. And, golly-gee, there just might be a couple of hours left over in the day for me to attend a class or two.''

He didn't looked convinced. "There are other considerations.''

Her gaze narrowed. "Actually, there aren't. I wasn't asking your permission, Sadik. I thought you'd figured that out last night. You can't buy me off and you can't change my mind. I have the feeling that I'm going to spend a lot of my life having to give in on other issues, but this one isn't negotiable. I suggest you get over it.''

With that she turned on her heel and stalked from the room. The man was thick as a post and just as unmovable. But she refused to be the one to give in on this issue. It was too important to her. Not only did she want to get a college degree, but she had something to prove to both Sadik and herself. They both needed to learn that she meant what she said.

She headed for the front of the palace where her driver was already waiting. Sadik would have a heart attack if he knew that this morning she even planned to take the wheel. Driving around town was the only way she was going to become familiar with her new hometown. If the heavens opened because a royal princess actually dared to have a life, then they were all going to have to get used to a little rain.

Sadik found it impossible to concentrate after Cleo left. He muttered something about difficult women, then went in search of his father. The man had been married several times. Obviously Hassan knew how to control women far better than his son.

"She cannot be reasoned with," he complained when he was shown into his father's private office. "She defies me at every turn. She is headstrong. I do not know how to bend her to my will."

His father leaned back in his large chair and motioned for Sadik to be seated on the opposite side of the desk. "If you insist a woman bend too far, you will break her spirit."

Privately Sadik thought that might improve the situation. "She is planning on attending the university. I do not understand why being my wife and the mother of my children is not enough for her."

"Have you considered that bettering herself is a far more productive way for her to spend her day than shopping? If she has interests, she'll be happy in Bahania."

"She will have our son to care for. That is interest enough."

His father shook his head. "It is not so simple, my son. I wish it were. Women can be complex creatures." He turned and stared out the window, at the formal gardens flourishing in the mild, fall temperatures.

"I do not want complex. I want obedient."

Hassan returned his attention to Sadik and smiled. "Then you should not have married Cleo."

"That's what she said."

"She is wise."

Not the words Sadik had been looking for. "Then you agree with her decision to attend the university.

You do not think I should forbid it.'' No point in saying he'd already tried.

"You must do as you see best in your marriage," his father said. "However, Cleo will not be dictated to without reason. She has already given in to you on the matter of getting married."

"She had no choice." Sadik was still bitter that Cleo had not been honored by his proposal.

"Exactly. Let her have a choice this time. Be wise, my son. Do not listen to your head as much as your heart."

"My heart has nothing to do with this."

The king shook his head. "The choice in that is yours, but I fear you will regret holding her back. How much of your concern about Cleo is that she will not have time to raise your children and how much of it is your fear that she will have a life away from you? One that she may come to enjoy more?"

Sadik ignored the questions, mostly because he didn't like them. He was a royal prince of Bahania—he feared nothing.

His father's phone rang. Sadik nodded and left. But he did not feel better for having spoken of his troubles. Uneasiness dogged him. Things with Cleo were not as he thought they would be. She was not grateful that he had married her, nor was she willing to do as he requested, no matter how reasonable the demand. She spoke of the university, and before their marriage she had even spoken of love.

He knew she wanted to take possession of his heart. That he could not allow. The price of love was loss. Losing Kamra had upset his world for many weeks, and although he refused to admit it to anyone but himself, Kamra had mattered far less than Cleo. He did not want to consider the destruction that would follow if his wife were to disappear from his life. He could not allow himself to be shattered that way, so he would not allow her to matter.

As he did every morning Sadik appeared promptly at seven forty-five. He carried a tray into the bedroom and set it carefully on the nightstand. He bent low and kissed Cleo on the mouth, then handed her the disgusting, purple protein drink he insisted she have each morning.

While she concentrated on sipping without gagging, he drew back the covers and pulled up her nightgown. He placed both his hands on her stomach and addressed her growing belly.

"Good morning, my son," he murmured, his voice low and filled with affection. "Today we will discuss the ways of the desert. The desert is like a magnificent woman who will not be tamed. Treat her with respect and she will serve you all your days. Ignore her or underestimate her and she will destroy you."

Cleo couldn't help smiling. "You underestimate me all the time and I have yet to destroy you. Although I do think about slapping some sense into you from time to time."

Sadik ignored her, although she saw the corners of his mouth twitch slightly.

"Your aunt, Princess Sabrina, was once foolish enough to go out in the desert by herself," he continued. "She was trapped by a sandstorm and nearly died.

You, my son, will never behave in such a manner. You and the desert will be one.''

Cleo choked down her protein drink and let Sadik's words wash over her. She didn't understand this morning ritual of his—mostly because she was sure their unborn child couldn't understand anything that was being said. But she enjoyed the time with her husband. When he was like this, so kind and gentle, touching her, caring about her and the baby, she believed they might have a chance at making their marriage work.

Unfortunately, more times than not, Prince Sadik was stubborn and uncooperative.

She finished her drink about the same time he finished his ''desert'' lecture. Sadik rose and sat on the side of the bed.

''What are your plans for the day?'' he asked.

''I'm meeting with my tutor.''

His expression tightened. ''You are too intelligent to require a tutor.''

She didn't know whether to laugh or scream. On the one hand he hated that she insisted on starting at the university; on the other, he was insulted that she would need help getting up to speed.

''Sadik, while I appreciate the vote of confidence, the reality is that I was never much of a model student. I barely made it through some of my high school courses. The university can't refuse me—I'm married to you. So to avoid embarrassment for everyone, I'm brushing up on a few subjects.''

Her husband's gaze suddenly narrowed. ''Who is your tutor and where will you be studying?''

For a second her foolish heart took flight. Sadik's

jealousy gave her reason to hope. But before she could read too much into the question, she reminded herself that he had made it clear he wasn't about to fall in love with her. So being jealous was a knee-jerk response, not one that meant anything.

"A woman," she said with a sigh. "Don't get your panties all in a bunch. Even I know better than to hire a male tutor."

"That is as it should be." He rose and kissed her again, then touched her cheek. "I count the hours until I see you later today."

She watched him leave. A part of her wished those words were true. He said them each morning, but they were simply a ritual without meaning. Like their marriage, she thought sadly, not knowing how to make things different. No matter how intensely she and Sadik made love, no matter how often, she couldn't seem to touch more than his body. She wanted to believe there was a way to reach his heart, but so far she had no bright ideas. Maybe it was time for some expert advice.

Cleo had never flown in a helicopter before. She tried to stay calm and not think about the insanity of trusting her life to a giant flying bug. Rather than give in to her fear, she stared down at the endless stretch of desert. Somewhere in the sandy beige of the Bahanian wilderness sat a secret city hidden for over a thousand years.

The City of Thieves acted as a home base for thousands of wandering nomads. The residents had originally made their fortunes by stealing from desert travelers. Eventually they had realized it was far easier to offer protection to the merchants on the Silk Road than to take from them. Now the nomads protected the vast oil fields belonging to Bahania and neighboring El Bahar.

Cleo had read up on the City of Thieves, at least on the legends about the place. The city didn't officially exist. In a way it was like Camelot—without the English accents.

Cleo smiled at her feeble joke, all the while trying not to feel apprehensive. Zara had returned from her honeymoon the previous day. As much as she wanted to deal with Zara over the phone, it didn't seem fair. Not after all they'd been to each other. Her foster sister would want an explanation, and Cleo was going to give it to her. Maybe in defining all that had happened between Sadik and herself, she would come to understand it more clearly.

The helicopter moved lower. Cleo squinted against the bright sunlight. There, at the base of a mountain, she thought she saw something. Buildings maybe? They blended perfectly with the surrounding rock. Was it possible that a medieval city still functioned in these modern times?

The original stone huts had given way to an elaborate walled city, complete with a castle. The location had been decided by two factors: the geography that allowed a stone city to blend into the surroundings and a river flowing from an underground spring. The water circled the city, then dove beneath the earth to be cleansed and renewed.

Sabrina's husband, Prince Kardal, ruled the city. Zara's new husband, Rafe, was in charge of security.

Although a Bahanian princess, Zara now called the City of Thieves her home.

Cleo pressed a hand against the window as the giant bug slowly lowered itself to the stone landing pad in front of the main doors to the palace. She could see vast fields, irrigated by the river, and corralled cattle and goats. In the distance several dozen nomads made their way back to the desert, after visiting the city.

Once the helicopter came to a stop, a uniformed guard opened the door, put out a step for her and bowed.

"Welcome to the City of Thieves, Princess Cleo," he said, straightening and offering a hand to help her down.

Cleo rested her fingers lightly on his palm. She stepped onto the worn stone and saw a courtyard filled with a busy marketplace. She had the sense of stepping back in time—as if life in the city had been like this for a thousand years. After all, it probably had. She half expected to see a dancing scarecrow and tin man singing about visiting a wizard.

But instead of Technicolor creatures, the main doors of the palace opened to reveal Zara and Sabrina. They both rushed toward Cleo and gathered her close in a group hug that brought tears to Cleo's eyes.

Zara stepped back first and glared at her sister. "Don't for a moment think I'm ever going to forgive you for running off and getting married without telling me about it."

Cleo winced. "I didn't want to spoil your honeymoon. Are you really mad?"

Zara sighed. "No. I understand." She looked at her

sister's bulging stomach. "It's not like you had a lot of time to wait. I just wish I'd been there."

"I would have liked that, too," Cleo admitted as the weepy feeling started to get stronger.

Sabrina slipped between them both and drew them inside the castle. "Now, ladies, there will be no tears today. And no ill tempers. We're going to have a fabulous 'girls only' day. We're going to stretch out on sofas and eat fattening food, while we trash our husbands and talk about shoes. Are we in agreement?"

Zara smiled at Cleo. "Yes. I agree. And I'm really glad you're here."

For the first time since her marriage to Sadik, Cleo felt as if she could actually relax. "I'm glad I'm here, too."

Zara and Sabrina took Cleo on a tour of the castle before they settled down for their girl talk. While sections of the ancient structure had been modernized, there were still rooms and corridors constructed of stone, with slits for windows and no heating, cooling or air-conditioning.

"There are fireplaces," Sabrina said as they strolled through a large guest bedroom. "The stone walls are thick enough to keep out the heat, and something about the way the place is built actually takes advantage of the night breezes to cool the place off. But you wouldn't want to get lost around here. It's big enough that it could literally take days to find you."

"I'm still using a map," Zara confessed. "I also have a cell phone that I've had to rely on more than once. It's pretty embarrassing to phone Rafe and tell him to come find me.''

Sabrina laughed. ''He hardly minds. You're still newlyweds.''

Zara sighed with contentment. ''You're right. He doesn't mind at all.''

Cleo smiled because she was expected to, but she couldn't help feeling a twinge of envy for Zara's and Sabrina's happiness. They were both married to wonderful men who were completely devoted. They were—

A tall man dressed in traditional desert robes swept around a bend in the corridor. Cleo froze, then instinctively took a step back before recognizing the handsome prince. He nodded at both her and Zara, then swept Sabrina into his arms.

''How are you?'' he demanded. ''Do you feel well? Should you be resting? Are you hungry?''

Sabrina lightly touched her husband's face, then stepped free of his embrace. ''Kardal—I'm great. Really. You've got to stop doing this.''

''You're my wife. Of course I'm concerned about you.''

''Yes, but if you make me crazy, I'll be forced to stab you in your sleep. Now get back to work.''

He kissed her fiercely, then spun on his heel and retreated.

Zara glanced at Cleo. ''Sabrina has a secret.''

The king of Bahania's youngest daughter shrugged as she led the way down the corridor. They entered a large living area with several sofas pulled up around a large coffee table overflowing with trays containing a traditional English tea.

Cleo was still caught up in Kardal's need to see his wife in the middle of the day. They had been married for almost two years. Should he be over that by now?

The envy she'd been feeling twisted in her chest, making her wish for things that weren't going to happen—at least not in her marriage.

Sabrina sank down on one of the couches and motioned for the other women to do the same. But instead of leaning back, she sat forward and stared intently at Cleo.

"I'm pregnant," she said.

Cleo had barely sat down, but she instantly sprang to her feet and hurried toward Sabrina. The two women hugged.

"I'm so happy for you," Cleo said genuinely.

At least she could say *that* without feeling as if she were lying. She *was* happy Sabrina was going to have a baby. They could discuss infants and pregnancy to their hearts' content without boring everyone else, and their children would grow and play together.

Tears glittered in Sabrina's eyes. "I'm about two months along. I didn't say anything when I first found out because there was so much other stuff going on, but I'm ready to let everyone know." She brushed at the tears on her cheeks. "I don't get it. I'm barely feeling any morning sickness, but I can't seem to stop crying."

"Hey, that happened to me all the time, too," Cleo said, returning to the sofa and plopping down. She glanced at Zara. "Feeling any pressure?"

Zara chuckled. "Maybe a little. But Rafe and I have talked about kids, and while we want several, we both would like at least a year with just the two of us. We want to travel and adjust to being married." Zara glanced around at the soaring thirty-foot ceilings and the eight-hundred-year-old tapestries on the walls. "Plus I have to get used to living in the City of Thieves."

"That's not a hardship," Sabrina said with a wave of her hand. "It's great here. To be honest, I hate being away from the castle." She leaned forward and began pouring tea. "Please help yourself."

Cleo eyed the table laden with all kinds of cakes, cookies, sandwiches and scones. There were also silver-trimmed glass bowls filled with different kinds of salad nestled on ice, and plates of fruit.

They discussed Sabrina's pregnancy. Cleo mentioned the name of the doctor she was going to see for her monthly checkup, and Sabrina talked about the possibility of seeing a midwife from the village outside the main castle. The whole time they talked, Cleo could feel Zara watching her. Finally she turned to her foster sister.

"You might as well tell me what's on your mind. You know you're going to say it eventually."

Zara tilted her head. She and Sabrina looked amazingly alike, with their long dark hair and big brown eyes. But while Sabrina was completely comfortable in her surroundings, Zara had the air of someone who expected to wake up from a dream at any moment.

"Are you happy with your life?" Zara asked.

The question surprised Cleo. It also made her choke as her herbal tea went down the wrong way.

Happy with her life? What was that? Cleo could recall specific events that had made her happy—an unexpected birthday party when she'd turned sixteen or a weekend trip with Zara. For her happiness came in measurements of hours, maybe even the occasional day, but never in terms of a life.

"I'm still adjusting," she said, hedging.

Sabrina didn't look any more convinced by her answer than Zara did. "How's my brother treating you?"

She thought about his daily attentions each morning, when he brought her breakfast and talked to their unborn child. She thought of the tenderness of his embrace, when he pulled her close to make love with her.

"He's good to me…in an arrogant-prince sort of way."

Zara and Sabrina exchanged a glance. "Then why are your eyes so sad?" her former foster sister asked.

Cleo set down her tea. Part of her wanted to tell the truth because she needed to talk to someone. She felt a little strange about confiding her deepest feelings in front of Sabrina, but the odds were that Zara would tell her, anyway. Besides, Sabrina knew Sadik—maybe she could offer advice.

"He cares about the baby," Cleo said slowly. "I know he has committed himself to the marriage."

"But?" Zara promoted.

Cleo put her hand on her round belly. "We didn't plan this. Once I went home, Sadik never bothered to get in touch with me. I'm not sure he would have ever thought of me again if I hadn't shown back up on his radar scope. He wouldn't have married me if I hadn't gotten pregnant.''

Sabrina set down her cup, as well. "I get it," she said sympathetically. "You're in love with him. I'm sorry I didn't see it before. I mean I should have guessed.''

Zara looked stunned. She glanced from Cleo to Sabrina, then slowly shook her head. "No, *I* should have seen it. Oh, Cleo, you went and fell for him, didn't you?''

For once her hormones seemed to be asleep because she managed to nod without breaking into tears. "I didn't mean it to happen. Obviously, he doesn't love me. He's still in love with Kamra—he told me so,'' she added quickly when Sabrina started to protest. "He gave her his heart, so he doesn't have it to share with me. I'm still trying to figure out what I'm supposed to do now. I asked the king if I could leave, but he won't let me.''

"Of course not," Sabrina said gently. "You're carrying his first grandchild. Any child I have will be heir to the City of Thieves, and Zara's children won't be in line for the throne. Besides, the king really likes you, Cleo. He's not going to let you walk away.''

"I found that out." She spread her hands, palms up. "So I'm trapped. I love a man who won't love me back. Maybe one of you would like to slap me and tell me to snap out of it. That or offer really good advice about how to make this work. I figure we're in the marriage for the long haul. I'd like to make it a happy relationship. If not for us, then at least for our children.''

There was a long, awkward silence. So much for brilliant advice.

Sabrina stood and moved around the coffee table. She sat next to Cleo and took her hand. "Don't give up on Sadik's heart. I saw him with Kamra years ago and the thing is, I don't remember anything. When they were together it was uninteresting. When you two are together sparks fly."

"At the risk of telling you more than you want to know, that's just about sex."

Sabrina grinned. "You've had sex?" She touched Cleo's belly. "No kidding. I think we're all aware of that." Her smile faded. "I meant what I said about Kamra. He never looked at her the way he looks at you. There's definitely something between you. If it's passion, then that's something to build on."

Sabrina squeezed her fingers. "Don't forget how my brothers were raised. There were virtually no mother figures around. They were shuttled off to boarding school at a ridiculous age. They don't know how to express their feelings. Sex may be all Sadik is capable of right now."

"But he loved Kamra." And he refused to love her.

"Did he love her?" Sabrina asked. "Or does he want to remember loving her? If he builds a shrine in his mind, then he gets to have happy memories. But what I remember is that she was spineless. I don't think she ever had an opinion of her own. She would have made him crazy in a matter of months."

"I make him crazy now."

"Maybe, but in the best way possible. Don't give

up. Not on him or your marriage. I think you have the potential for something amazing.''

Cleo desperately wanted her sister-in-law's words to be true. Given her current situation, she didn't have any choice but to hope.

Chapter Thirteen

At four that afternoon Sabrina and Zara walked Cleo to the entrance of the palace. Cleo could hear the approaching helicopter in the distance. She supposed that transportation-on-demand was one of the "princess perks." It beat having to travel to the City of Thieves by car...or even camel.

"Just let me know when the childbirth classes start," Zara was saying. "I'll be there. Once you get close to delivery, we'll have a helicopter standing by. When you're within a week of delivering, I'll move into the palace."

Cleo hugged her sister close. "I know Rafe is going to hate me for taking you away from him, but thank you for offering to be with me. It means a lot."

"Rafe understands," Zara promised. "Besides, if he

gets lonely, he can always come spend the night with me.''

Sabrina touched her own still-flat stomach. ''My big request is that you both lie about how bad childbirth is. I want to hear happy, pain-free stories. Don't tell me about screaming or blood or anything icky.''

Cleo laughed. ''You got it. You'll get the made-for-TV version.''

As the helicopter touched down, Sabrina and Zara promised to be in touch soon. Cleo waved goodbye, then headed for her ride. As she approached the buglike vehicle, she was surprised when the door opened and a familiar, tall man stepped down.

Flying in the face of common sense and all that was reasonable, her heart skipped into overdrive. It was as if the silly organ hadn't figured out it was foolish to fall for a man still in love with someone else. But despite the lecture, Cleo couldn't help but be happy at the sight of her husband.

He hurried toward her.

''I came to escort you home,'' he said, bending down to kiss her lightly, before taking her hand in his. ''Had you told me you wished to visit your sister and Sabrina, I would have come with you this morning.''

Startled, she couldn't help asking, ''Why?''

''So you would not make this journey alone.''

Cleo thought about the pilot and copilot who had accompanied her. She'd hardly been by herself. ''I was fine.''

He frowned at her. ''You are my wife. I expect better than 'fine' for you.''

She wasn't sure what to say to that. Rather than

speak, she allowed Sadik to help her into the helicopter. He fastened her seat belt, then settled next to her. Once they were airborne it was difficult to speak over the engine and the whipping of the rotors, but Cleo didn't mind. It was enough to be next to Sadik, holding his hand.

Maybe Sabrina had been right. Maybe there was a chance that they could make it work. After all, the precious ghost of Kamra might still have possession of his heart, but it could not give him a child. A child would be a strong bond between them.

Cleo vowed then and there to release the past and her pain about his lingering affection for his late fiancée. Instead she would focus on all that was positive between them. They were going to have a child. Sadik had promised to be a supportive and faithful husband. They enjoyed each other's company and there was great passion between them. Somehow she would make that enough.

Cleo pushed aside her dinner plate and reached for the wallpaper sample book.

"Sadik, you have to be practical. Despite your claims to the contrary, the baby *could* be a girl."

Her husband of two months dismissed her with a flick of his hand. "I am a prince of Bahania. I only have sons."

"While I can appreciate that, you do know it's not your decision." She shook her head when he would have interrupted. "I know that technically the father determines the sex of the child. My point is, you don't get to pick which sperm decides to do the happy dance with my egg. What if it was a girl sperm?''

Instead of answering, he simply stared at her. No doubt his point was that as he was a Bahanian prince, his girl sperm would have the good sense to stay behind the boy sperm, thus ensuring the birth of a male child.

She gave a mock sigh of surrender. "Fine. We'll assume the baby is a boy. But on the one-in-a-million chance that it's a girl, I would prefer we not pick trains and airplanes for the border print. Either we find something neutral or we wait until the baby is born.''

They sat at the dining-room table in their suite, having just finished dinner. Sadik still wore the suit he'd put on for work, but he'd removed his jacket and pulled off his tie.

Now he reached across the table and took her hand in his. "Whatever you would prefer, Cleo. If you like your teddy bear paper, then that is my wish, also.''

She wasn't surprised by his statement. In the past few weeks, they'd both gone out of their way to defer to the other person's opinion. She supposed they were figuring out how to make their marriage work. Once she'd given up on the idea of having Sadik love her, everything else became easier. He was supportive, attentive and affectionate. Whenever she got a knot in her stomach or thought how much better things *could* be, she reminded herself that this was enough.

"Bears it is,'' she said, opening the sample book to that page and writing down the order number. "I'll call about it in the morning.''

"I can have my secretary order the paper.''

She smiled. "By the time I explained what I want, I could have just as easily called the company myself." She flipped to another page on the pad. "Also, we have to coordinate what day we want the baby's room painted."

"I remember. You pick the most convenient day and I will arrange for us to use one of the guest rooms for the night." He rose and drew her to her feet, then kissed her lightly on the mouth. "I do not want you breathing in the paint fumes. We will stay in a guest room until the paint is dry and the smell is gone."

She knew there was no point in arguing. The baby's room was on the other side of the suite, and she doubted the paint would bother her. Still, Sadik was being sweet, and she didn't want to discourage that kind of behavior.

He led her to the sofa in the living room. When she settled herself on the soft cushions, he sat on the coffee table in front of her and lifted one of her feet onto his lap. Strong fingers massaged her arch. As he rubbed away her tension, she let her head fall back.

"You do that very well," she murmured.

"I read about it in one of my books."

She opened her eyes and glanced at the stack of books on pregnancy that Sadik had ordered from the Internet. He hadn't simply ordered them—he'd read every word and he'd remembered what he'd learned. He was constantly spouting off information she didn't know. Of the two of them, he was far more mentally prepared to have the baby than she was.

"Circulation is most important for the pregnant woman," he said matter-of-factly. "It is why I encourage you to sleep on your side and not on your back. There is a large vein that returns blood from your lower body. When you sleep on your back, you cut off that route. You must use your body pillow.''

"Yes, Sadik," she said meekly.

He raised his eyebrows. "You say the words, but I do not think you agree with the seriousness of the matter.''

"When you're doing that to my toes, it's hard to take anything seriously.''

He responded by changing the subject. "Have you chosen the furniture yet? It will all have to be made by hand, so there is not much time.''

They'd pored through dozens of catalogs, along with visiting local baby boutiques. "I'm leaning toward using antiques that are here in the palace. The king showed me some of the things placed in storage last week." She smiled. "Maybe I can find your old crib.''

He placed one foot on the ground and reached for her other leg. "I would prefer our son not be forced to use my old castoffs.''

"They're not castoffs. They have sentimental value.''

"Not to me.''

"You were a baby. You can't remember.''

"I recall enough. You may use any antiques you wish but not things I had as a child.''

Sadik could be difficult and arrogant and stubborn, but except for the topic of their baby's gender, he was almost never unreasonable.

She pulled her foot free of his touch and leaned toward him. "I don't understand.''

"I know."

She reached toward him, but before she could touch him, he rose to his feet and stalked to the far side of the room.

"Sadik?"

"I ask that you not argue with me on this matter."

"If it means so much, I promise I won't look for anything that belonged to you. But I don't understand why you're being so insistent."

He stood by the French doors leading out to the balcony that encircled that level of the palace. The sun had long since set and they hadn't pulled the drapes, so as he gazed at the glass all he could see was a reflection of the room. Cleo stared at that same reflection, trying to read her husband's expression.

"Are you angry?" she asked.

"No." He shoved his hands into his trouser pockets. After what felt like several minutes, he turned to her and drew in a deep breath. "Some time ago you told me of your past. How you had grown up in poverty, with a mother who was rarely around."

She nodded.

"You were surprised that I did not judge you or find you wanting. You were surprised when I admired your strength for overcoming the conditions under which you had been born."

"I remember."

"I am Prince Sadik of Bahania, second-born son to King Hassan. I am the master of my fate."

She smiled gently. "I've actually heard that speech before."

"I know. Sometimes I say it to make myself believe it is so."

What was he talking about? "There's no question of you being the king's son."

"Agreed. I do not fear being branded illegitimate. My parents were married." He returned to the sofa and sat down next to her but not touching. He didn't look at her. "My father had two great loves in his life. Zara's mother, and Reyhan and Jefri's mother. His first arranged marriage produced my older brother, Murat, and his second produced me. There was no love lost in either case. Murat's mother died in childbirth, and my mother killed herself rather than be with him. Or me."

All the blood rushed from Cleo's head, leaving her feeling as if the room had begun to spin. Her heartbeat sounded loud in the silence. She struggled to find words.

"What happened?"

"She took pills. I was still very young and did not realize the significance of what she had done for some time. It does not matter."

But of course it mattered. Cleo knew it mattered very much, although she couldn't say exactly how.

"So you were left alone?"

He shrugged. "My father was king. He had affairs of state. There were nannies for a time, then I was sent off to school when I was seven."

Cleo might not have a drop of royal blood in her veins, but she knew what it was like to grow up lonely. She couldn't fix Sadik's past, but she could promise him that history would not repeat itself.

"When I was very young, I swore that no matter what, I would never abandon my child the way I'd been abandoned," she told him. "No matter what, Sadik, I will be there for our child."

"As will I."

Sadik stared into Cleo's beautiful face and saw the conviction blazing in her eyes. At that moment, as they shared their vows, he felt closer to her than he had ever felt to anyone. He had never shared the horrors of his past before. His brothers knew, of course, but they did not speak of such things. He had never talked of it with his father. Yet the information was all there, in the back of his mind. The knowledge that his mother could not have been bothered to stay alive to be with him for the first few years of his life.

He told himself he was a grown man and such events from his past had no meaning. Most of the time he believed the words.

He shifted on the sofa and held out his arms. Cleo came to him instantly. She snuggled close, her growing belly pressing into his side. He accepted her comfort, enjoying the heat of her body and the way her small hands clung to him.

Her nearness made the ghosts of the past fade as his body responded to her curves and her fragrance. Desire filled the empty places inside of him. But he did not reach for her. Not yet. Instead he waited, wanting her to be the one to reach for him.

Over the past few weeks he had seen a change in Cleo. She no longer demanded that he love her. The word never passed her lips. He had seen her trying to make their marriage a success and he did his best to improve things between them. Yet despite her smiles and easy laughter, he sensed there was something missing. When he touched her in bed, she was always willing, yet she never touched him first.

He did not mind seducing her each time. Seducing Cleo was the stuff of dreams. But he knew there was still a wall between them. Sometimes he thought even *she* did not realize there was something wrong. Because he knew her so well—the sound of her breathing, the beat of her heart—he could not likewise be fooled.

She was like a boat cut adrift on a slow-moving river. At first she seemed to simply hang there, but eventually she would slip away. He wanted to reach out and grasp the rope, pulling her in. He knew the problem and he knew the solution. She wanted him to love her. Love.

Why did she seek the one thing he could not provide?

And then, because he could not resist her any longer, he reached for her. She responded instantly, kissing him with a fervor that took his breath away. As he pulled her into his arms and carried her into their bedroom, he told himself that the boat hadn't drifted out so very far that day. Perhaps the tide would turn and she would come to rest in a place she would never want to leave.

"Our holiday celebrations are unique," King Hassan said as he and Cleo strolled through his garden. "We celebrate many faiths in our country, and each is given its due. You will find much of the old city decorated as if for a large party."

He motioned to a bench in the shade of several palms. It was a frequent stopping place for them on their twice-weekly walks.

Cleo settled on the stone bench and rested her hand on her belly. Based on her growing girth, she found it difficult to believe she still had over two months left.

"As long as I can have a Christmas tree for the suite," she said, smiling at her father-in-law. "I love the smell of pine."

"Something we do not have here in our world." He nodded. "I have already arranged for the palace to be a winter wonderland, specifically for your pleasure."

His kindness made her feel all weepy inside. "You're spoiling me."

"I enjoy the process. Besides, you are the honored mother of my firstborn grandson."

Cleo had thought that Hassan's attention to her might drop off once he found out that Sabrina was pregnant, but so far that had not happened. Perhaps he actually liked her for herself. Since returning to Bahania, she'd spent much time with the king. While he still had the power to make her incredibly nervous, she enjoyed his company and their times together.

"Tell me of your studies," he said as he leaned down to pet one of the palace cats that strolled along the path.

Cleo shifted to get comfortable. "They're going really well. I figure that realistically I won't actually be taking classes at the university until next fall. When the baby comes, I want to be free to get used to being a mother. But until then, I'm working hard. I actually have three tutors now."

Hassan raised his eyebrows. "How many subjects are you…" He frowned. "What is the phrase?"

"Brushing up on."

"Ah. That is it."

Cleo shrugged, feeling vaguely guilty. "Well, it's gotten a little more complicated than that. Alice was my first tutor. She helps me with my general knowledge and study habits. I'm learning how to read a textbook and understand the central points and how to take notes. She started talking to me about Bahanian history. I found it really interesting, but she doesn't consider herself an expert, so one day a week I see Luja. She's lived in the old part of the city all her life. She's got to be close to a hundred. Anyway, she knows practically everything about Bahania, so we talk about history and politics."

Hassan touched her hand. "I am most proud of you, child."

Cleo ducked her head. "Yeah, well, I'm doing it because it's interesting."

"Learning about your new homeland is most wise. And who is your third tutor?"

"That's the funny part. Alice was going over some basic math stuff with me and I found I really liked it." Cleo shook her head, still amazed by what she was discovering about herself. "The thing is, I'm also really good at it. So she's brought in a math tutor. Shereen is taking me through basic algebra and next up is geometry. I can't wait."

"So Zara isn't the only smart one in your family."

"I guess not." Hard to believe but true, she thought happily. All those years ago she'd never given school a chance. How would her life have been different if she'd found even one thing to be good at? Maybe she wouldn't have made so many stupid choices in her personal life.

"And my grandson's room is ready for his arrival?"

Cleo didn't even bother correcting Hassan's assumption about the baby's gender. She'd grown tired of fighting that particular battle. She just hoped she was focused enough to enjoy the moment should her baby turn out to be a girl.

"We're nearly done," she said, then laughed. "Technically the room is completely empty, but we've ordered what we need, and I've chosen several pieces from the palace warehouse. Those things are being cleaned."

She and Sadik had spent a fabulous day strolling through a massive building stuffed with Bahanian treasures. She had been careful to avoid anything from Sadik's past as she didn't want to spark painful memories. Even now, when she recalled what he'd told her about his mother, she felt a knot form in her stomach. How could a woman just turn her back on her child? Not that her mother hadn't done the same sort of thing.

Maybe that was why she found it so easy to love Sadik. On the surface they were nothing alike, but underneath they were very much the same.

Hassan touched her face. "I see a trace of sadness in your eyes. You are thinking about my son."

His announcement should have startled her, but she'd grown used to the fact that her father-in-law could be very perceptive.

"I am content," she said quietly. "He's a good man

and a caring husband. He is eager for our child. We enjoy each other's company. There is respect. Isn't that enough? To want more is to wish for the moon.''

"How dark the night sky would be without the light of the moon."

"But she travels on her own path and cannot be ordered to appear."

He smiled. "You are learning the ways of the desert."

She was learning because every morning Sadik spoke lovingly to their unborn child, teaching him or her about the ways of Bahania. She supposed he was as much a tutor for her as any of her other instructors. From him she had learned about the lineage of the famed Bahanian stallions, and how to tell if the birds circling in the sky told of water nearby.

"The desert is now my home," Cleo reminded the king. "I must learn her ways and respect them."

"What of the sadness in your eyes?"

She didn't want to think about that. "In time it will fade."

"Because you will come to love him less?"

She wasn't surprised that he had guessed her secret. How hard could it have been? "In time I will get used to the situation."

"Will you get used to him not loving you back?"

The blunt question made her wince. "Yes." Because she didn't have a choice. She refused to live her life being unhappy. "In time the friendship and respect will be enough for me."

Hassan frowned. "My son is a fool but not an idiot.

In time he will see the treasure he holds cannot be replaced.''

''Maybe.''

Cleo wasn't confident that Sadik would ever be willing to let go of his past. The memory of Kamra was too important to him. And as long as the ghost of his late fiancée had a hold on his heart, he would never be able to offer it to her.

The nurse motioned for Cleo to step up on the scale. Cleo kicked off her sandals and thought light thoughts as she did as requested. The digital number rose upward at an alarming rate, causing her heart to sink in direct proportion. When it finally stopped, she stared, unable to believe anyone her height could actually weigh that much.

''Dr. Johnson is going to have my head on a platter,'' she muttered as she slipped back into her shoes. ''She warned me on my last visit not to gain more than a pound a week.''

Sadik dismissed her concerns. ''You are a vision of health and beauty. If your blood pressure is normal, then Dr. Johnson will not be concerned.''

''Uh-huh.''

Cleo was not convinced. She knew that the combination of stress and fabulous palace food had her eating a whole lot more than she was supposed to. She followed the nurse into the examining room and gingerly shifted her body onto the table.

The nurse put the cuff around her arm and began pumping in air. A minute later she released the cuff and announced that Cleo's blood pressure continued to be in the excellent range.

"That's something," Cleo muttered, still bracing herself for the lecture. Unfortunately, she didn't have long to prepare.

One of the advantages—or disadvantages, depending on the day—of being a member of the royal family was that one did not linger in doctor waiting rooms or examining rooms. Dr. Johnson, a tall, blond woman in her late forties, entered on the heels of the nurse leaving. She studied the chart attached to a clipboard, then raised her head to look at Cleo.

Cleo instantly felt like a two-year-old caught with her fingers in the cookie jar. Only, in her case it had been a lot more than cookies.

"I know," she began. "You said a pound a week, which would mean four pounds, right? But it's seven. I've been trying to be good."

Sadik bent over and kissed her mouth. "Enough. You need not explain." He smiled at the doctor. "Her blood pressure remains normal and there is no edema in her hands and feet. I check them daily for swelling."

Dr. Johnson looked impressed. "You're a most attentive father-to-be, Your Highness."

Sadik nodded. "Cleo is my wife. She carries my son. What could be more important than her well-being?"

When he talked like that, Cleo got all tingly inside. She knew he didn't mean it the way she wanted him to, but as she'd decided several weeks before, she was determined to make what she had with Sadik be enough.

Dr. Johnson sighed. "You're right, Your Highness.

But a few less calories each day would improve her well-being.'' She turned her attention to Cleo. ''Your urine sample is fine, as well. No excess sugar. You're doing great.''

''If getting a little chubby.''

Sadik picked up her hand and kissed her palm. ''You remain, as ever, a goddess.''

''I wish my husband said that to me,'' Dr. Johnson muttered, then grinned. ''Guess I should have fallen for a prince, huh?''

Cleo smiled weakly, as she took the paper gown the doctor handed her. She wasn't sure she would recommend handing one's heart over to a member of the royal family—it wasn't a recipe for happiness.

Five minutes later she'd undressed and draped the paper gown over herself. As she climbed back onto the table, Dr. Johnson wheeled the ultrasound machine into place.

Sadik hovered through the routine exam. Dr. Johnson explained about uterus size and baby placement while Sadik fired off several questions. They all listened to the steady beat of the baby's heart, then the doctor squirted warm gel onto Cleo's belly in preparation for the ultrasound.

Cleo turned so she could see the monitor. Sadik moved close, taking her hand in his.

''All right. Let's check out the royal baby,'' Dr. Johnson said as she moved the wand over Cleo's stomach.

Images began to form. Although Cleo had seen her growing infant before, her heart quickened at the sight of the tiny body thriving inside of her. She caught her breath and clutched Sadik's fingers tightly in her own.

"There's the head," Dr. Johnson said, pointing at the screen. "Spine, arms, legs. Now if we can just get the royal prince or princess to move slightly, we can determine the gender." She glanced up. "You did want to know, right?"

Sadik shrugged. "We know. Our child will be a boy."

Cleo rolled her eyes. "Yes. I would love to know if you see anything. Despite my husband's insistence, I'm not convinced of anything yet."

Dr. Johnson shifted position, trying for another angle. "I see shadows, but nothing definite. Sorry. It's impossible to tell."

Cleo stared at the screen. "It doesn't matter," she said softly. She reached out to touch the image. "As long as the baby is healthy and growing, that's all that's important."

Fifteen minutes later they were on their way to the waiting limo. Sadik had his arm around her, pulling her close. Cleo welcomed his attention.

"Isn't it amazing?" she murmured when they were seated on the smooth, leather seat. "Every time we see the baby, I can't believe it's real." She placed her hand on her stomach. "Life is such a miracle."

"Our miracle," Sadik told her, resting his hand on top of hers. "Our child."

His dark eyes burned with a fire that made her heart race. In that moment they shared something more profound than being married. Together they had formed a new being. Wonder didn't begin to describe what she felt, but she saw the answering emotion on Sadik's face. She reached for him at the same moment he drew her close.

Chapter Fourteen

Sadik's mouth was firm and passionate, his lips an inescapable seduction. She supposed that, as pregnant as she was, she shouldn't want to make love with her husband, but she couldn't help responding to his desire...or her own. Dr. Johnson had said they could keep being intimate until she told them otherwise.

Sadik breathed her name. His long fingers traced the curves of her face, even as he deepened the kiss. Their tongues stroked and circled. Low in her belly she felt the familiar tension.

The drive back to the palace had never been so long. Despite the raised privacy partition separating them from the driver, she knew that nothing more than kissing would happen until they reached their rooms.

Somehow the anticipation made everything even more intense.

Finally they arrived back at the palace. Giggling like teenagers, they raced through the hallways of the palace, heading for their private suite. Sadik opened the door, then quickly drew her inside.

They were pulling clothes off each other, even as they moved toward the bedroom. He touched her everywhere, arousing her to the point of frenzy. When they sprawled onto the bed, they quickly found their way into the side position they'd been using for the past few weeks. It allowed them to face each other while they made love, without having to worry about her growing belly.

Cleo arched in pleasure as he moved into her. His arousal filled her completely. One of his hands stroked her intimately, making it impossible to keep from gasping in delight. They stared at each other. She studied the handsome face that had become so familiar to her.

"We're having a baby together," she whispered.

His slow, happy, proud smile touched her heart. "I know," he told her, speaking softly. "I saw him today. We both saw him."

Yes, she thought even as passion overwhelmed her. They *had* both seen the baby, and that connection bound them together for life.

He moved his hand faster and she lost herself in her release. Sadik soon followed, calling out her name and clinging to her. When they were finally able to catch their breath, he stroked her face and traced the outline of her mouth.

"You are my wife," he said. "I am your husband. And so we will be until we die."

A simple truth, she thought. Inevitable. Why had she been avoiding the inevitable? Her heart swelled with her feelings until she had no choice but to voice them. She kissed his mouth.

"I love you, Sadik."

He froze, as if he had suddenly been cast in stone. Then his eyes darkened and he pulled her against him.

"I am glad," he said. "That is as it should be. You will love me well, and now you will be content to stay."

He continued to talk, but she couldn't hear the words. She didn't think she was even capable of breathing. Had her heart stopped? Had *she* been cast in stone?

Eventually Sadik rose and dressed. He urged her to rest for the afternoon, and because she couldn't move or speak, she didn't argue. Instead she lay under the covers he'd pulled up around her and stared at the ceiling. Eventually something warm and wet trickled down her temple into her hair. She touched the spot, only to find tears.

An awful pain filled her chest. Hopelessness overwhelmed her. In that moment, at the doctor's office, she had opened her heart to Sadik in a way she'd never opened to anyone before. She'd allowed her love to grow until it overwhelmed common sense. On a rush of feeling, she'd handed over her heart. And he had taken it without offering anything in return.

Cleo knew she'd lived through more disappointments than many people. Her mother's continual abandonment, both emotional and physical, had left her scarred. Her teenage search for love, when she'd been foolish enough to think that sex was the answer. Her mistake in judgment with Ian. All those events had wounded, bringing her to her knees, but she'd always been able to get up, figure out what she'd done wrong, learn from it and start over. For the first time in her life she felt defeated.

She couldn't win this battle, because the enemy was a ghost. Sadik would never love her. It didn't matter how much respect they had between them or how many children bound them together. He would never love her.

Until this moment she'd avoided the truth. Now that she faced it, she wasn't sure what she was supposed to do.

Three days later Cleo realized that her continued weight gain wasn't going to be a problem. She didn't want to eat, she couldn't sleep and every inch of her body ached as if she'd been dropped from a three-story building.

She forced herself to choke down food because of the baby. For the same reason, she went to bed each night. But while Sadik slept, she stared at the ceiling. As for the pain…she knew it was simply the physical manifestation of her broken spirit. She had played a high-stakes game and she had lost.

In the cool of the morning she walked toward the garden where she was due to meet the king for their time together. She'd dressed in a bright-blue dress and had applied more makeup than usual in an effort to disguise her distress. She even managed to smile at the sight of the king of Bahania being batted at by two calico kittens.

Hassan heard her step and glanced up. He smiled in welcome, then set the kittens on the ground and rose from the bench. His expression changed from pleased to angry in the space of a heartbeat.

"What is wrong?" he demanded by way of greeting.

Apparently she hadn't done such a great job of concealing her distress. "Nothing. I'm fine. I haven't been feeling that well in the past couple of days. I think I have a touch of the flu."

Hassan cupped her face in his hand and stared into her eyes. "Child, you are a constant delight to me. However, you are not an accomplished liar. What I see in your eyes has nothing to do with the flu. Tell me what troubles you."

His concern was more than she could resist. Unwelcome tears filled her eyes. She closed her eyes and spoke the truth.

"I'm dying inside," she whispered. "Please, Your Highness, don't make me stay here."

The king led her to the bench. After she was seated, he handed her one of the kittens. Cleo stroked the soft fur and felt sharp claws dig into her hand. The small body was warm. When the kitten nestled onto her palm and leaned against her chest, a low rumbling purr burst forth. The sound was far too big for the baby creature's size. Through her tears she smiled.

"She's very beautiful," she said as she stroked the kitten's head.

"She has much spirit, that one." Hassan sat next to

her and picked up the other kitten. "Her mother isn't purebred like most of my cats. She is not a particularly good hunter, but there is something about her heart. She loves with all her being." He shifted the kitten in his arms so he could stroke its belly. The kitten collapsed with delight.

"This will be her last litter," he said. "Each time her kittens grow and we give them away, she suffers greatly. For weeks she is sad. Sometimes she will not eat and I must feed her by hand." He shrugged. "No one has told her that I am the king."

"It sounds like she wouldn't care."

He chuckled. "Probably not. After all, that makes her a royal cat." His humor faded. "As much as I love her kittens, for they carry a piece of her with them, I cannot bear to put her through the pain of having her litters leave her again. Her unhappiness wounds me."

He looked at Cleo. "She is just a cat. You are the daughter of my heart. Every day you are gone, I will bleed a little inside. I will think of you often. In time we will need to come to some arrangement with regard to my grandson. But for now you are free to go."

She hadn't had a clue where he'd been going with the cat story. Now that he'd given her permission to flee Bahania, the band tightening around her chest loosened a little and she was able to draw in air. Time away from Sadik would allow her to recover…or at least start the healing process. She had a bad feeling that he was going to be the only man she ever really loved.

But she would deal with that reality another time. For now it was enough that she could retreat and lick her wounds in private.

"Thank you, Your Highness. I know this isn't what you want. It's not what I want either, but—"

Hassan held up a hand to silence her. "I'm giving you time, Cleo, not a permanent pardon. You and Sadik will have to deal with each other eventually. But for now a separation may be the best thing. We have a villa in Florida. As we approach the beginning of winter, that will be a safe place for you. I will arrange for a doctor to be on call for you there. The plane will be ready for the journey at three this afternoon. Does that suit you?"

Actually it overwhelmed her. She put the drowsy kitten on the bench, then flung herself at the king. He held his kitten in one arm as he hugged her with the other.

"I am sorry to see you go," he told her. "You have been a wonderful daughter. I am very proud of you, Cleo. Never forget that. As for Sadik, I am sad to say, my son is a camel's ass."

Sadik paused in the act of typing in a transfer order. The cursor blinked at the tail end of a multimillion-dollar entry. His fingers hovered over the keys, but something had distracted him.

He raised his head, wondering if he had heard an unfamiliar sound. No. It wasn't that. He tried to shake off the feeling of something being wrong and return to his work, but he could not. He finished typing the number, hit Enter, then saved his work and exited the computer program.

After rising, he crossed to the window and stared out. No unexpected storm darkened the horizon, yet he couldn't shake the feel of tension in the air. Something was different…and very wrong.

Cleo.

He left immediately for the private wing of the palace, but even before he entered their suite, he knew she was gone. Even so, he crossed the living room and headed for the bedroom. Most of her clothes hung in the closet, but a few casual pieces were gone, as were her cosmetics. He checked the nightstand by the bed and saw that her vitamins were missing, as well.

Cursing under his breath, he hurried toward his father's office. Was it too late? No, he told himself. Wherever she had gone, he would find her. He had to find her. The pace of his heart picked up the rhythm of the words—he *had* to find her.

He entered the king's office without knocking. One of the guards took a step forward, and a secretary rose to his feet, but Sadik ignored both of them. He headed directly for the double doors and entered without knocking.

King Hassan sat behind his desk. He didn't seem surprised to see his son, and waved off both the guard and the secretary before motioning for Sadik to take a seat.

Sadik dismissed the invitation with a shake of his head. He approached the desk and placed both hands on the broad surface.

"You told her she could leave."

He spoke the statement rather than ask the question. His father met his angry gaze with a steady look.

"Yes, I did."

Sadik curled one hand into a fist and pounded it on the desk. "You had no right. She is my wife."

Hassan rose and glared. "Her heart is broken. I would not watch her fade away from unhappiness. You did not recognize the treasure you possessed, so now you have lost her."

No! It could not be so. Sadik sucked in a breath, but the act took great effort. Perhaps because there was suddenly a gaping hole in his chest.

"She was content. She loves me. She told me herself."

Just three days before. He remembered the moment with perfect clarity. For the first time since he had found out about the baby, he had been sure that Cleo was not going to bolt. In the act of confessing her love, she had freed him to relax. If she loved him, she would stay. They would always be together. Women who loved were happy. It had always been so.

"Apparently loving you is not enough," Hassan said angrily. "She expected more, as did I."

Sadik frowned. "What more would you expect? I have been a faithful and caring husband. She wants for nothing. I attend to her every morning, I have learned all I can about her pregnancy and the upcoming birth."

His father slowly shook his head. "You have not learned the most important lesson. I thought you would. I knew what you went through after Kamra's death, and I know what you vowed. But you are wrong, Sadik. You have always been wrong. Not loving someone does not keep you safe—it merely keeps you alone."

He resumed his seat. "I will do nothing to help you.

Cleo is leaving. After the birth of my grandson, we will fly to see her and the baby. Only then will we discuss what is to happen.'' His father's gaze narrowed. "My intent is not to keep you from your son. However, Cleo needs time. I forbid you to follow her."

Sadik left without responding. His own father had turned against him. And Cleo had run from him. He took a step, then another, only to stop when he felt a sharp, angry pain in his chest. He could not breathe, could not think, he could only endure the hollow emptiness filling him.

The sensation was faintly familiar. He searched his memory and recalled that he had felt it when he had lost Kamra. But that pain had been a pinprick compared with the open wound he experienced at the loss of Cleo. It was as if he'd been ripped in two. How could there be a world without her? How could he survive? She was both sunlight and moonlight in his ever-dark sky. She had accused him of only caring about the baby, but she had been wrong. The child was an unexpected gift—she was his everything.

He forced himself to keep walking. Memories flashed through his brain, each more accusing than the last. How he had taken her affection and her love for granted. How he had never told her what she desperately needed to hear. He'd been so sure he could avoid pain by not admitting his feelings, but the words did nothing to change how he felt inside.

"Cleo."

He breathed her name. The act of speaking it aloud gave him strength. He knew what he had to do.

He ran through the corridors of the palace. The

shortest path to the garage led through the public areas, and he raced through a tour in progress. He heard the surprised tour guide identifying him to the tourists, and the whirring clicks of dozens of cameras snapping his picture.

Once in the rear of the palace, he hurried into the garage and got behind the wheel of his fastest car. There was not much time. Cleo would be leaving on the family jet, so he couldn't count on an airline delay to keep her in Bahania.

He raced down the circular drive that led into the city. A flash in his rearview mirror caught his attention. Guards in pursuit!

He ignored them and put his foot on the gas. Fifteen minutes later he entered the highway that would take him to the airport.

Hurry. Hurry. Hurry.

The words beat inside his brain, over and over. He tapped his fingers against his steering wheel and willed his car to go faster. In the distance he heard the sirens of the guards after him, but he ignored them. Nothing mattered but finding Cleo.

After five minutes he decided he had better call ahead and see if he could delay her plane. Several frustrating minutes later, he was no closer to getting in touch with the tower than he had been before he had started. His father sought to block his attempts to bring Cleo home. He would have to—

Sadik slammed on the brakes. Tires screamed in protest, the car shimmied, then bounced as he drove it onto the shoulder. His chest squeezed so tight, he couldn't breathe.

A black car—like the ones used by members of the royal family—lay on its side in a ditch off the highway. Several rescue vehicles crowded around the damaged automobile. It was as if time had bent and circled around itself to bring him back to a moment he had already endured. He had found Kamra in just this way.

Dead on the side of the road.

He brought his car to a stop. Had he been able to speak, he would have screamed out his protest. Indescribable agony tore through him. He wanted to demand justice. He could not live without Cleo. Didn't anyone understand? How could she be gone?

He did not know how long he sat there. It felt like lifetimes had passed, but perhaps it was only a few minutes before a police officer knocked on the window of his car.

"Prince Sadik? Is there a problem?"

Sadik lowered his window and slowly shook his head. "The accident," he rasped in a voice that sounded a thousand years old. "The passenger."

The officer consulted his notebook. "Someone from one of the embassies. He was drunk, of course. Fortunately he only hurt his car and his pride."

Sadik stared at the man, unable to absorb the words. "He? Not a woman?"

"Just one person in the vehicle, sir."

Sadik tried to thank him, but he didn't know what he said. All he knew was that Cleo was not dead. He still had a chance. If he was too late at the airport, he would travel the earth until he found her. He *would* bring her home—whatever it took to convince her.

He pulled out onto the road. The guards from the

palace were much closer now. He could see their cars in his rearview mirror. The police officer jumped back as Sadik sped down the highway, sending gravel flying.

In a matter of minutes the airport was in sight. He circled the main terminals, heading for the private hangar that housed the royal fleet. Up ahead he could see one of the cars from the palace pulling to a stop in front of the small terminal. Behind, the guards gained ground. It would be close.

He floored the accelerator, racing to the terminal. Up ahead Cleo stepped out of the car, then turned toward the noise. Sadik raced as close as he dared, then slammed on the brakes, turned off the engine and sprang from the vehicle.

"Cleo, you must wait," he yelled as he ran toward her. Behind him a dozen or so guards gave chase.

He was close enough to see the pain on her face and the confusion as she registered that he was being pursued by palace guards.

Cleo stared at the spectacle of her very proper, very *princely* husband flying toward her as if the hounds of hell were at his heels. Obviously, he'd figured out she was leaving and expected to stop her. She didn't know what he wanted, but she knew she was too heartbroken to listen to any logical argument about how they had to stay together for the sake of their child.

"Cleo, please."

She turned her back on him and headed for the terminal. If she hadn't stopped by her doctor's office to make sure it was all right for her to fly, she would have been gone by now. His last-minute theatrics wouldn't have mattered.

The sound of a rifle cocking caught her attention. Cleo froze, then shifted so she could see Sadik. She nearly stumbled in amazement.

Prince Sadik of Bahania, the king's second oldest son, stood in the grasp of several armed guards. He put up a good struggle and a fourth man joined the fray in an effort to keep Sadik in place. A fifth man aimed a rifle at the prince.

"We have our orders, Your Highness," the armed guard said. "You are not to interfere with Princess Cleo in any way."

Cleo blinked. This couldn't really be happening. Not to her. Since arriving in Bahania, she'd seen some crazy things, but this was…insane.

Obviously, she wasn't going to have the clean getaway she'd wanted. Sadik was here and determined. She would have to deal with him.

She dropped her carry-on bag to the ground, then walked toward her husband. The fact that it took four guards to hold him still was fairly impressive, not that she would tell him so. She looked at his handsome face, at the mouth that had kissed hers so tenderly. In that moment she wished with all her heart that things could have been different between them. She would have changed the rotation of the earth for him…if only he had loved her back.

"I'm not going away forever, Sadik," she said softly, trying to ignore the guards standing so close. "I need time to think and to make peace with my life. I know that we're going to have a child together. You and I will have to come to terms with that and with how we're going to raise our child. The king has given me a reprieve, not permission to disappear.''

He stared at her with an expression she'd never seen before. The intensity of his gaze made her uncomfortable, as did the guards. She turned to the one with the rifle.

''Any chance you'd let him go?''

The guard stunned her by nodding and stepping back. Instantly Sadik was free. Cleo blinked.

''I did that?'' she asked.

Sadik stepped away from the guards and straightened his suit jacket. ''Apparently my father gave them orders to follow your instructions. I am grateful you did not ask to have me shot.'' He took her hand in his and led her toward the terminal. ''If you will permit me a few minutes of your time before you leave?''

She was still too amazed by what had happened with the guards to protest. It was only when she found herself in a small, private room that she realized Sadik was going to try to convince her to stay. She sighed. When would he figure out that all the sensible words in the world weren't going to work on her? When would he see that—

''You are alive,'' he breathed, pulling her close. ''I thought I had lost you, both when you left and then again when I saw that car on the side of the road. I could not have lived without you.''

He wasn't making any sense. She wiggled to get free of his embrace. ''Sadik, what are you talking about?''

He cupped her face and rained kisses on her skin. Once his lips brushed hers, it was darned hard to maintain emotional distance. She forced herself to push him away.

"I'm not falling for that again," she told him, taking a step back.

"You do not understand." He grabbed her upper arms. "I thought you were dead. I thought it had happened to me again. Only this time the horror was greater, so much greater because once you were gone, I knew that I would have lost the most precious part of myself."

She resisted the urge to shake her head. "You're not making any sense. Gone where? On the plane?"

He kissed her. She tried to stop him and then, well, she stopped trying. Because as much as she knew she had to leave Sadik, she didn't want to go.

"I have hidden the truth," he murmured against her mouth. "I thought if I did not confess it, even to myself, that it could never hurt me. I refused to say how I felt about you. And by not acknowledging my feelings, I planned to keep you at arm's length."

His dark eyes brightened with emotion. "Losing Kamra pained me. The discomfort was an inconvenience. Losing you would destroy me, Cleo. You are my world. So I pretended not to care. Because if I did not care and you went away, I should not mind."

She swallowed hard. "Sadik?"

He stroked her hair away from her face. "I love you, Cleo. I cannot exist without you. This isn't about our child—it is about you. Only you. From the beginning you have entranced me. Those first few passionate days together changed me forever. But I was determined to resist. I would not be ruled by a mere woman."

She heard the words and desperately wanted to believe them. Mostly because she didn't have a choice. "So that's why you didn't call or try to get in touch with me when I went back to Spokane? Because I was a mere woman."

He smiled slightly. "I had something to prove to myself."

"And did you?"

"No. Spending all my time trying *not* to think of you is exactly the same as thinking of you all the time. I knew you would return for the wedding, so I vowed to wait. I was also determined to have you." He kissed her palms. "In my bed and in my life."

She leaned against him and let his healing words wash over her. "Can you really let Kamra go?"

He sighed. "She has been gone a long time. I used her as a talisman to hold you at bay. The truth, my love, is that she was an arranged match. We came to some agreement between us. There was mild affection, but to compare my feelings for her with my feelings for you is to compare a glass of water with the ocean. I love you."

She flung her arms around him, burrowing close. It was something of a trick, what with her stomach in the way.

"Please stay," he begged.

She closed her eyes, as much to hold in the joy of the moment as to try to compose herself.

"I will love you forever," he promised. "I will prove myself to you every day. I swear on my honor, you are the most important person in the world to me. You belong here, with me. Please, Cleo."

She could not stand to see her handsome prince brought to his knees. She kissed his mouth.

"I will stay," she told him, her heart filled with happiness. "And I will love you...one year for each grain of sand in the Bahanian desert."

Epilogue

Tired but happy, Cleo held her newborn daughter to her chest.

"You see," Sadik said, ever the proud papa as he strutted through the enormous private room in the hospital. "A girl. I said as much from the beginning, and I am always right."

Cleo looked at Sabrina and Zara. All three women rolled their eyes.

"You said it was a boy," Cleo reminded her husband, even as she nearly floated from happiness. "I was the one who kept saying our baby might be a girl."

"No. You do not remember the sequence of events." He moved to the side of the bed and touched his daughter's cheek. "She is lovely. Just like her mother."

Despite the lingering discomfort from the delivery, Cleo couldn't remember a more perfect moment in her life. After years of never fitting in—of always being on the outside—she'd finally found a place to belong. Who would have thought that would happen in a palace?

It was all because of Sadik. Not a day went by without him confessing his love a dozen times. He could not be more attentive or affectionate or loving. At times he was still the arrogant prince, but Cleo found that part of him kind of growing on her. Princes were not always easy to be married to, but there were plenty of rewards.

He kissed her forehead. "My wife, you are to be honored among women."

She laughed. "I'd settle for a soft pillow to sit on and some sleep."

Hassan burst into the room, trailed by two of the princes. "I have congratulated the doctor on delivering my first grandchild. I believe she was relieved."

Cleo figured Dr. Johnson had felt just a little bit of pressure when she'd gone into labor.

Hassan approached the bed. "My perfect granddaughter." He slapped Sadik on the back. "A girl—just as we discussed."

Cleo settled back into the pillows. "Your father and grandfather are big, fat liars," she cooed to her baby. "Yes, they are."

Hassan and Sadik chuckled. Then the king turned to Reyhan, his third son. "Both your sisters are pregnant. Sabrina is due in six months, and Zara the following month. You have not yet taken a wife. I believe it is time. I shall arrange a match.''

Reyhan, as tall, dark, handsome and arrogant as his brothers, cleared his throat. Cleo was surprised to see that the prince actually looked uncomfortable.

''That will not be necessary, Father.''

Hassan frowned. ''You must be married. We need more heirs.''

Reyhan cleared his throat again. ''Yes. I understand. However, there are circumstances...''

The room grew incredibly silent. Even the baby seemed to be listening. Reyhan shrugged. ''There was a young woman in college. While I have not seen her in six years, the truth of the matter is that we are... already married.''

* * * * *

Look for Susan Mallery's exciting new short story,
THE SHEIK'S VIRGIN,
part of Silhouette's
THE SHEIKS OF SUMMER *collection,*
in August 2002.

**Where royalty and romance
go hand in hand...**

The series continues in Silhouette Romance
with these unforgettable novels:

HER ROYAL HUSBAND
by Cara Colter
on sale July 2002 (SR #1600)

THE PRINCESS HAS AMNESIA!
by Patricia Thayer
on sale August 2002 (SR #1606)

SEARCHING FOR HER PRINCE
by Karen Rose Smith
on sale September 2002 (SR #1612)

And look for more Crown and Glory stories in
SILHOUETTE DESIRE starting in October 2002!

Available at your favorite retail outlet.

If you enjoyed what you just read,
then we've got an offer you can't resist!

Take 2 bestselling
love stories FREE!

Plus get a FREE surprise gift!

Clip this page and mail it to Silhouette Reader Service™

IN U.S.A.
3010 Walden Ave.
P.O. Box 1867
Buffalo, N.Y. 14240-1867

IN CANADA
P.O. Box 609
Fort Erie, Ontario
L2A 5X3

YES! Please send me 2 free Silhouette Special Edition® novels and my free surprise gift. After receiving them, if I don't wish to receive anymore, I can return the shipping statement marked cancel. If I don't cancel, I will receive 6 brand-new novels every month, before they're available in stores! In the U.S.A., bill me at the bargain price of $3.80 plus 25¢ shipping and handling per book and applicable sales tax, if any*. In Canada, bill me at the bargain price of $4.21 plus 25¢ shipping and handling per book and applicable taxes**. That's the complete price and a savings of at least 10% off the cover prices—what a great deal! I understand that accepting the 2 free books and gift places me under no obligation ever to buy any books. I can always return a shipment and cancel at any time. Even if I never buy another book from Silhouette, the 2 free books and gift are mine to keep forever.

235 SEN DFNN
335 SEN DFNP

Name	(PLEASE PRINT)	
Address	Apt.#	
City	State/Prov.	Zip/Postal Code

* Terms and prices subject to change without notice. Sales tax applicable in N.Y.
** Canadian residents will be charged applicable provincial taxes and GST.
   All orders subject to approval. Offer limited to one per household and not valid to
   current Silhouette Special Edition® subscribers.
   ® are registered trademarks of Harlequin Enterprises Limited.

SPED01   ©1998 Harlequin Enterprises Limited

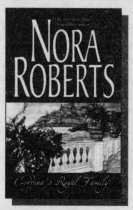

COMING NEXT MONTH

SPECIAL EDITION